THE BOAT R

THE BOAT RACE MURDER

BY

R. E. SWARTWOUT

Ostara Publishing

First Published Grayson & Grayson 1933

Every reasonable effort has been made by the Publisher to establish whether any person or institution holds the copyright for this work. The Publisher invites any persons or institutions that believe themselves to be in possession of any such copyright to contact them at the address below.

ISBN 978-190628800-6

A CIP reference is available from the British Library

Printed and bound in United Kingdom

Published by   Ostara Publishing
                   13 King Coel Road
                   Lexden
                   Colchester
                   CO3 9AG

CHAPTER ONE

A dismal afternoon was closing in on the river. The tide was on the ebb, and the broad, gleaming stream swirled and eddied in a vast curve, with warehouses and factories on one side and a high, bare bank on the other, and spanned by the towering ironmongery of Hammersmith Bridge. On the stream, far in the middle, floated a solitary racing eight.

The eight was the latest product of an ancient firm of boat-builders: a brand-new ship, built on the latest scientific principles, and hewn from the same cedar log which provided that other brand-new ship which, in ten days' time, was to contend with its sister in a trial of speed from Putney to Mortlake; a fratricidal contest, since both strokes had rowed together in the Eton eight, and both crews were coached by men who had rowed together, as Old Blues, in a Leander crew of ever so long ago; and since both crews, with their coaches and presidents, were united in a last-ditch stand against the Unorthodox style of rowing; and, finally, since both crews were indissolubly at one, with their respective universities behind them, in opposition to the theory, advanced in a certain newspaper read by no gentleman, that the Boat Race was merely capitalist dope, calculated to distract the attention of the workers from the class war.

The ship, whose nose was pointed down-stream, came to rest in the middle of the river, opposite the huge bulk of the furniture repository. A long white motor-launch overtook the eight and halted a few yards away. It contained three men: the driver, a young man who sat silent at the wheel; an elderly man in an ulster and cloth cap, an experienced waterman whose task was to look after the coxswain; and, finally, a red-faced man who stood in the bows of the launch, clad in an overcoat and a light blue cap: this was the coach.

"Cox, you little blighter!" shouted the coach, when the launch came alongside. "Didn't you hear me say 'easy'?"

The cox, looking like a wretched little rat huddled up in his thick blazer and scarf, shook his head.

The stroke, a slim, fair-haired young man, glared at him as he adjusted his scarf. "Listen to what he says, you beastly little pip-squeak!" he hissed.

"Shut up, Alan," snapped the coach. "This is my job. Look here, you chaps," he went on, leaning over the side of the launch, "cox or no cox, that was an awful bit of paddling. It simply won't do, ten days before the race. Alan, you simply mustn't hurry them like that."

"Silly fool!" muttered stroke.

"Shut up, stroke," came sharply from five, the President.

"I want you to row from Hammersmith Bridge to the Mile Post," the coach continued. "A good hard row—but for God's sake, Alan, remember this isn't a bumping race. Don't take them off at forty. You haven't got a crew to pace you, but I want a hard, steady row, and with this stream you might break the record. Put the wind up those Oxford beggars. Turn round, cox."

Stroke unwound his scarf, and tossed his fair hair with an impatient gesture. "Steady row!" he grumbled. "How the crazy idiot expects me to——"

"Shut up, there!" cried the President. "Get on with it, cox."

Stroke shrugged his shoulders; but cox, tautening his little body, cried out: "Back her, bow side! . . . Easy . . . Paddle on, two and four! . . ." and the long ship swung round with the tide, preparatory to its last ten-minute burst down to Putney.

The boat-house: a ramshackle, brick and timber edifice, built for utility and not for comfort: downstairs, in the exiguous cavern provided for the purpose, the ship has been laid, dripping, to rest on its trestles, and now the faithful Willie Edwards busies himself about it, as he has done these thirty years past, while his assistants carry in the long oars, and stack them against the rafters, and bolt the massive doors; up the outer stairs, to the changing rooms, tramp the crew, eager for rest and warmth after a long afternoon's outing.

"Migawd, what an outing!" said Jack Ramsey, the diminutive but alert bow, as he threw himself on a hard bench.

"Full marks for frightfulness," agreed Kirkpatrick, who rowed four, and whose beefy rotundity had earned him the nickname of "Bonzo."

Tom Scorby, number six, slowly peeled a half-soaked sweater from his vast frame, and morosely spoke:

"The more I see of Mr. Blasted Strayler, the less I like him. Rushing the stroke up like a—like I don't know what, and turning round and cursing old Selfridges' and me every five strokes for not being thought-readers and knowing what he's going to do next. Sick of it, I am."

The spare man now entered from the sitting-room, and eyed the Blues sardonically.

"Jolly boating weather!" he remarked. "Had a good outing?"

"Oh, lovely," said number three. "Went right up to Barnes in a drizzle, then on the way back cox didn't easy us in time, so we had to turn round and go back to Hammersmith to start a row, then Alan took us off too fast, and we got ragged, and Horace made us turn round *again* after a minute and a half, and re-start. You're lucky not to be with us, Owen, old man."

"Lucky!" said the spare man. "I don't know about that. At any rate, you blokes are companions in misfortune. Here am I, training as hard as any of you, on the off chance of somebody catching measles or sudden death, pottering about all by myself in a beastly little sculling-boat, with never a word from anybody, with no reward, and with no nice little blue coat to wear like you."

There was a moment's embarrassed silence, broken by the cox.

"Cheer up, Owen," he said. "I'll sell you my place if you like. Then you can see what fun it is, being nagged, nagged, nagged at by Alan all day long. 'Cox, you little beast, why don't you tell them to keep her level? Cox, keep your head still! Cox, you're out of the tide! Cox, why can't you listen?' It's like that every day, and, I can tell you, I'm fed to the back teeth."

"And don't I know it!" cried Owen, bitterly. "Didn't I have four weeks of rowing behind him, till he went and had hysterics in Horace's bosom, and got me kicked out?"

"Buck up, you blokes!" said Harry Westlake, number two, in a forced effort to restore cheerfulness. "After all, we broke a record to-day."

"Record, my foot!" The speaker was a tall, slim young man, whose raven hair and dark complexion suggested southern blood. "Nice sort of record," he went on. "It was a put-up job, to try to make us feel happier. You noticed that Horace chose an afternoon when the press launch was following Oxford, so that there should be no Nosy Parkers with stop-watches about? And that he chose a finishing-point where the river is about a mile wide, with no mark at all except a little notice-board on the tow-path ? So naturally, when the hand of his watch was a second short of the record time, he sang out 'Easy, cox!'—and who was to swear that we weren't more or less opposite the post when he shouted ?"

"I expect he and Alan cooked it up between them," observed Tom Scorby. "Typical Etonian trick."

"Shut up, Tom," said Ramsey, in half-simulated anger. "I don't love Alan any more than you do, but I won't have that from a damned Harrovian who took up rowing for the good of his health!"

The discussion was cut short by the abrupt entry of the President, Robert Tatersale, who had been talking over the afternoon's work with the coach. He was a short, stocky young man, with a thick neck and a John-Bull-like countenance which betokened a strength of character developed to stubbornness. He was followed into the room by the lanky form of the stroke, Alan Strayler, who drooped lackadaisically on to a bench with a weary sigh. Tom Scorby grunted, and made room for him, ostentatiously withdrawing his damp sweater and zephyr.

"Grousing as usual," said the President, unwinding his long blue scarf, honourably faded by the wind and spray of three Putney seasons. "I believe you'd grouse, Selfridge's, if you went to Heaven and were asked to row in the Archangels' Eight, on the glassy sea. What's the matter now?"

There was a brief silence, which Bonzo ventured to break with: "Rather feeble outing, we thought."

"Oh!" said the President, pulling off his sweater. "Says you, as the saying goes. It may interest you to know that Horace says that considering the tide there hasn't been anything better since the 1924 crew. And several of the Old Men said the same thing."

The crew silently divested themselves of their wet rowing clothes, and drifted one by one to the next room, where the showers were. The President laid his hand on the stroke's shoulder and said, in a low voice: "Time's getting short, you know. Things have got to get better——"

At that moment the cox approached the pair.

"Look here, Robert," he said, timidly, "I spoke to Tim Southward after the outing, and he said I wasn't across the tide that time opposite Chiswick Eyot."

Robert Tatersale turned swiftly and snapped at him with unwonted acerbity. "Don't answer me back. You were across the tide. Horace knows what he's talking about."

"Infernal little cox," murmured the stroke.

"And remember," went on the President, "there are plenty more coxes in Cambridge. You haven't got your Blue till you've steered in the race, you know."

CHAPTER TWO

As had been their custom for many years, the Cambridge crew had rented a house near the top of Putney Hill; a large, completely detached, redbrick house, with a few yards of gravelled drive and shrubbery in front, and a good-sized lawn, useful for croquet or stump-cricket, at the back. It had this special advantage, that there was a multitude of bedrooms upstairs, so that only four members of the crew were obliged to share rooms; moreover, there were two bathrooms. Downstairs the crew enjoyed a dining-room and a small drawing-room, on either side of the entrance hall, and a large room, containing a billiard table, overlooking the garden at the back. It was in this latter room that they were now taking their ease, an hour after the events last chronicled.

A Billiards Championship competition had been arranged; and Ramsey and Westlake, both complete rabbits at the game, were nominally fulfilling their part in the tournament, knocking the balls about the table in a happy-go-lucky manner. The others were scattered about the room, reading books or newspapers.

Click-click went the balls.

"I say, Tom," said Westlake, excitedly shaking the knee of the bulky number six, "I've potted the white. Is that a winning or a losing hazard? I always forget. And what does it score?"

Tom Scorby groaned, and put down his book. "I've told you infants often enough, it isn't done amongst gentlemen. You ought to apologise very humbly when you do it. And don't do it again. I'm trying to read a book."

Westlake took careful aim, and shot. His ball rolled swiftly across the table, and plumped resoundingly into the top right-hand pocket. "Do I get anything for that?" he inquired.

"Shut up!" said Scorby. "A bloke's done a murder, and I'm trying to find out how he did it."

"A murder?" asked Leopold Salvago, the dark young man, laying down his *Evening Guardian*. "If it weren't for the inconvenience of being caught, I shouldn't mind a nice quiet murder, on a night like this. The silly idiot who wrote this article, for instance—says we were hopelessly outclassed by the Ibis scratch crew on Monday."

9

"That all?" grunted Bonzo Kirkpatrick. "I sometimes feel like slaying the whole outfit of us—present company excepted. Either that, or suddenly throwing away my oar, standing up in the boat, and screaming."

"Well, don't do it now," said Salvago. "You can wait till the race, if you like. Then, when the race has started and we're all sure of our Blues, and Oxford are half a mile ahead, you can do it."

"Dry up, Selfridge's," came the voice of the President sharply, whose keen ears had caught this fragment of dialogue from the far end of the room. "If you keep on being a ruddy defeatist, we shall have to turf you out. Oxford are going to be half a mile behind, not in front."

"All the same, it would be a bit of a boon to the newspapers," remarked Hugh Gawsell, the cox. " 'Boat Race Sensation: Beefy Cantab Screams, Upsets Boat. "I did it in protest against Government's foreign policy," he says in exclusive inter-view.' "

"After which he wrung the cox's neck and threw the body over Hammersmith Bridge," continued Kirkpatrick, whereupon a brief scuffle ensued.

"And that *would* excite the newspapers," broke in Peter Lightfoot, number three. "A juicy murder on top of the Boat Race would be their dream of bliss. The newspaper reporters we see are such miserable little beggars—let's do it, just to make them happy."

"The only question is, who shall it be?" said Bonzo.

Leopold Salvago hummed softly to himself:

"As it seems to be essential that a victim must be found,
I've got a little list—I've got a little list."

"So have I," shouted the President, "and you're first on it, Selfridge's!" *Click-click-plop.*

"I've made a cannon, and then the red went down," interjected Ramsey. "What do I get for that?"

"You're next on the list," said the President.

"Hear, hear," said Scorby. "Shut up, you blokes, and leave me to my murder. They've found a chap in the shrubbery, with his face horribly mutilated, and I can't quite see how it happened yet."

"Is his cousin strongly suspected?" inquired Gawsell.

"No; but his brother is."

"Simpler still. You'll find," said the learned coxswain, "that the brother who's supposed to have been murdered really murdered the other brother, and let it be supposed that the other brother had murdered the brother who was supposed to be murdered—if I've got it wrong, you see what I mean. That *always* happens when, you have a corpse that's bashed about the face."

"You seem pretty familiar with corpses, cox," said Salvago.

"Of course I am. I'm a budding young surgeon. And how do you expect me to bud if I don't manhandle Corpses at meaters? My boy, I know a spot on your neck which if I squeezed, ever so gently, you'd fall down in a fit and never wake up till you found I'd cut you into little bits."

"We'll cut *you* into little bits, cox," said Scorby, "without any squeezings of the neck, if you don't dry up. Tell me this. This ruddy corpse had a revolver in his hand—I can't think why—and it went off all by itself when the hero-bloke arrived, and the hero loosed off *his* revolver, like a silly ass, and they all thought . . . Well, never mind that, but how did it happen?"

"Rigor mortis," answered the cox. "Sets in about three hours after death. Revolver put in his hand. Muscles contract, and the gun pops off. Stale old dodge."

"Silly idea," broke in Owen Lloyd, the spare man. "Like all these detective stories. The murderer sits up with towels round his head, concocting the most elaborate schemes which only come off provided that it's a foggy day, and provided that the 4.42 from King's Cross is two minutes late at Hitchin, and provided that the gamekeeper does what he's expected to do and calls the police at once. . . . Bah! If you want to kill a man, blip him over the head on a dark night when nobody's looking, and there you are."

"Pardon me, but there you're not," said the President. "Not in training, *anyway.*"

"Not even to-night?" said Salvago, in a pleading voice. "We've broken a record, and pleased all the Old Men, so we *might* be allowed a nice little murder."

"No," said the President, firmly. "I certainly feel like murdering most of you blokes, and I dare say you all want to murder me, not to mention Horace and Alan. But, if you don't mind, we'll leave all that until after the race. After all, I am President of this mouldy outfit, and I want to go down in history as having won a race. So, if it's not inconveniencing you too much, we'll just beat up these Oxford beggars first of all, and then we can play at detectives to our hearts' content. . . . Is that the new Freeman Wills Crofts you're reading, Tom?" he inquired.

"No," replied Tom Scorby. "It's a thing called *Death in the Dark,* by a bloke called Aloysius Adamson."

"I know," said Lloyd. "Chap who wrote *The Finger of Fate,* and *The Stain on the Bath Mat* Sort of imitation of Ronald Knox. You've *got* to know the whole of Bradshaw by heart, and have a mind that works like a Torquemada crossword, before you can begin to understand what it's all about. Give me something simple."

"Most of these detective stories are too simple," observed Hugh Gawsell. "You start with a country-house party. The third footman rushes in and says, in perfect B.B.C. English: 'The body of a well-dressed man has been discovered on the lawn. Circumstances point to foul play.' Then a detective——"

"——from Scotland Yard," broke in Salvago, "who, by a happy coincidence has been spending his holiday in the neighbourhood, investigates at once."

"Exactly," said the President. "Detectives, in fiction, never have real holidays. If Inspector French goes off to the Aran Islands to fish, he's sure to run into a murder."

"If I were a detective," said Scorby, laying aside his book, "I should go to China or South America, where one murder more or less doesn't matter."

"Exactly," went on Gawsell. "In this case, we have about a dozen well-defined suspects. The gamekeeper was heard to threaten Sir John a few days before the tragedy occurred. Jereboam Wildersnack, the dead man's cousin, profits heavily by his will. Thodoric Bulpit, another cousin, thinks he profits under the will, but doesn't. The behaviour of Major Bloodstock and Miss Gangle-mire, the governess, is so erratic as to merit immediate suspicion. And, of course, the strange demeanour of the butler is highly suspicious. And there you are."

"And of course the family solicitor, who hardly appears at all, really did it," concluded the President.

" 'When you have eliminated the impossible, whatever remains, however improbable, must be the truth,' " quoted Lloyd, with a grin.

"Utterly false reasoning," said Gawsell. "Who is to say what is impossible? I might say that it was impossible for Alan Strayler to get through an outing without cursing somebody, and without collapsing artistically over his oar, protesting that he was 'weak as a kitten,' but still . . ."

"Shut up, cox!" cried Robert Tatersale sharply. "Remember what I told you."

"And when you do eliminate the impossible," Salvago went on, "you have, probably, half a dozen improbables left you. Then where are you, Sherlock?"

"Observation," replied the spare man. "I deduce that you came straight up to the house without buying an evening paper. Why? Because if you had bought an evening paper at all you would have bought the *Piccadilly Gazette,* since you are a Socialist, and the P.G. is the only London Socialist evening paper; and you didn't buy it, because if you had bought it you would have read it, and if you had read it you would have seen the article by Jim Lowe which said that number seven was the best oarsman in the Cambridge crew, and if you had read that you would be in a good temper, instead of being in a foul temper as you are now. Q.E.D."

"Rot," said Salvago, indignantly. "I admit I haven't seen that evening paper, but if I were to slit your nasty great white throat for you, buying newspapers wouldn't help you to find out who did it."

"Oh, dry up, all of you," cried Scorby. "I'm trying to read a perfectly innocent detective story, and you'll all make me dream of cut throats and bashed faces all night."

At this moment Alan Strayler, the stroke, wandered into the room. He drifted across to the piano; and, sitting down, swept the long hair from his forehead before stretching his hands over the keys, to evoke a mournful cadence, which suggested clods of earth falling in measured blows upon a coffin. The Blues stirred uneasily.

"I say," interrupted Salvago at last, "must we have the Dead March in Saul? We're gloomy enough already."

"Dead March!" muttered the musician, without ceasing. "Handel's *largo.* Silly fool." And the dismal tones continued to roll majestically about the room.

Abruptly the door opened, and a head was thrust in.

"Cox!" said the head, sharply. "Come here."

Hugh Gawsell threw down his book, and passed quickly out of the room.

The owner of the head was revealed as an elderly man, clad in a mustard-brown suit, with a big head plentifully supplied with iron-grey hair, a benevolent face, and spectacles. This was Lewis Bethell, who had coached the crew in the earlier stages of practice, and who had now come down to see what his colleague, Horace Lampson, was making of things. He had rowed in a Cambridge crew an inconceivable number of years ago, and he still haunted the University in the guise of a history don.

Bethell beckoned the cox into the small drawing-room. In it sat Horace Lampson, the present coach, a stocky, red-faced man, with a small moustache, and with 'army' written plainly on his countenance. A fire burned briskly in the grate, and a couple of empty tumblers on the table showed that the two coaches had had recourse to something more stimulating than the official tea and biscuits of training. Bethell motioned the cox to a seat, and closed the door.

"Well, cox?" asked Lampson.

"Well?" echoed his colleague. "How are they?"

"Pretty well," answered the cox, fidgeting with the button of his blazer. "Nothing, to mention."

"All quite happy?" pursued the don.

"Happy enough. They weren't as pleased as they might have been about making a record."

"Why?" asked Lampson, sharply.

"Well," said Gawsell, "somebody—I forget who—" (diplomatically, for the coxswain knew perfectly well) "—suggested that it was a put-up job."

"Indeed," observed Bethell, pulling at his pipe. "And are they a happy family apart from that?"

Gawsell tugged at his button, stared about the room for inspiration, and finally answered: "Not entirely. Some of them are a bit fed up with Alan, what with one thing and another."

"Who?" asked Lampson.

Bethell laid down his pipe, and held a hand up. "Don't ask him that," he said, "it isn't fair. I think I know." He turned to the cox. "That will do, cox," he went on. "If they ask anything, you can tell them that Horace and I are very pleased with the crew's work. Eh?"

"Certainly," said Horace Lampson. "And tell them that since they broke a record to-day we shall have a fizz night."

The coxswain, eager to be released, rose and trotted across to the billiard-room.

CHAPTER THREE

"Half-past seven, sir."

Hugh Gawsell grunted, pulled the bedclothes tighter about his shoulders, and lay still.

"Half-past seven, sir. Mr. Tatersale won't be pleased if you make the gentlemen late."

"Confound you, Jelks," said the cox, opening his eyes. "What's it like?"

"Chilly, sir," said Jelks, with relish. "And a slight drizzle. There will be a strong wind on the river to-day, sir."

"Oh, go away, Jelks. You're about as cheerful as a sick headache."

The servant softly retired, and the cox crawled out of his tiny bed. He pulled over his pyjamas a sweater and a pair of the thick blanket-trousers which are the regular wear of a 'varsity crew in training, slipped his feet into tennis-shoes, and bundled a flannel scarf about his neck. So attired he issued from his bedroom and roused the other members of the crew in succession. His own small room was on the second floor, where also dwelt Ramsey and Bonzo Kirkpatrick in one room, and Westlake and Lightfoot in another. Having wakened them, he descended to the floor below, where the rest of the crew each had a bedroom to himself. After much groaning and rubbing of eyes the crew, dressed like the cox, assembled in the hall. Robert Tatersale came down the stairs, with as much briskness as he could assume on such a raw, depressing morning.

"What a crew!" he remarked. "You had two glasses of fizz last night, and you look as though you were recovering from the effects of Belshazzar's Feast. Are we all here? Where's——"

Gawsell plucked the President by the sleeve, and drew him aside.

"When I went into Alan's room just now," he said in a low voice, "he wasn't there. I thought I'd better tell you quietly."

"Not there?" said Robert, incredulously. "Where was he, then?"

"I don't know. His bed was tossed, but it didn't look as though it had been slept in."

The President sighed. "What on earth's the silly beggar been doing ? Keep quiet about it for a bit. Now, you chaps," he added in a louder voice, "out we go!"

"Where's Alan?" asked Lightfoot.

"Still snoring, I expect," said the President. "Lazy devil. Come on!"

15

The crew tumbled out into the road, trotted briskly for a few hundred yards up a deserted side street, and, turning, sprinted sharply back to the gates. As they clumped up the stairs Gawsell turned aside and tapped on the door of the coach's bedroom.

Major Lampson was sitting up in bed, reading a morning paper, with a cup of tea beside him.

"Come in!" he said. "Good morning, cox. How are they this morning?"

Gawsell hesitated.

"Well, they seem all right—what there are of them."

The coach laid down his paper. "What there are of them?" he echoed. "Good Lord, man, don't talk riddles before breakfast. What do you mean?"

Gawsell revealed what he had already told the President. Major Lampson gave a low whistle.

"This is about the limit!" he said. "Do any of the others know? You told Robert, I suppose? Where is Robert? Why doesn't he come in to see me?"

The cox went out, and in a minute returned with the President.

"What on earth is all this, Robert?" asked the coach. "You know what cox told me?"

"Yes. I've just been to Alan's room. The bed was certainly rumpled, but it wasn't warm, and I don't think it's been really slept in."

The coach threw up his hands with an exasperated gesture. "I suppose the silly fool climbed out of the house when we were all asleep, and went off on some spree in London. I've heard of spare men doing that sort of thing, when they were sure they wouldn't be wanted to row, but for stroke to do it, ten days before the race, is inexcusable. If he turns up this morning, you can tell him to pack up his things and clear out. I don't want to see him again."

A sudden thought struck him.

"Cox," he went on, "cut along to his room and see what clothes of his are missing. Then we shall know for certain."

Hugh Gawsell softly closed the bedroom door behind him. The landing was full of a swarm of young figures, some in pyjamas, and some with no clothing save a bath-towel wrapped round the waist, all moving towards the two bathrooms. He made his way to the stroke's small bedroom, which overlooked the garden at the back of the house. The bed, as the President, had said, was tossed, but it was cold, and it lacked the deep indentation which one would expect had it been slept in throughout the night. Over a chair were thrown negligently the light blazer, the white

16

flannel trousers, the white flannel waistcoat trimmed with blue, and the stiff shirt, which the missing man had worn at dinner the previous evening. In a corner stood three pairs of shoes; a pair of evening pumps, and two pairs of brown walking shoes. Opposite the bed was a wardrobe, the door of which Gawsell opened. In it were a light blue blazer of four thicknesses of flannel—the usual day wear of the crew—a brown lounge suit, a suit of evening clothes, and two pairs of blanket trousers. Next to the wardrobe stood a chest of drawers. This, on examination, revealed the normal collection of shirts, collars, handkerchiefs, ties, pyjamas, and underclothes. Nothing appeared to be missing. Moving to the wash-hand stand, Gawsell found the usual assortment of shaving tackle, soap, toothbrush, and sponge. Under the bed were two large suit-cases, of the sort which is supposed to expand almost indefinitely. Both were locked. Gawsell pulled both of them out, and shook them. Both were light, and apparently empty.

The cox, puzzled, surveyed the room.

"Here's my chance," he said, half-aloud, "to do some detective stuff. Something's wrong here—now, what is it?"

He strode to the corner where the laundry-basket stood, removed the cover, and looked inside. Two shirts, three collars, three handkerchiefs, and two pairs of socks.

" A couple of shirts, and a collar or two," hummed the cox, scratching his head. "Something's gone wrong. And a ring that looked like a—Got it!" he said, softly. "Pyjamas! That gives it away!"

And, still humming the refrain from Trial by Jury, he left the room.

Immediately outside, he collided with Leopold Salvago, whose lanky brown form was most insufficiently draped in a small towel.

"Hullo, cox," said the latter. "Trying to wake Alan up ?" He paused, and peered into the empty bedroom.

"Not there!" he went on, in a surprised tone. "But where is our dear Alan, then? Has he gone to town on a binge—broken training, to put it vulgarly? Don't answer if you don't want to—but, now I come to think of it, I seem to remember that you whispered some secret message into Robert's shell-like ear this morning. Was that it?"

Gawsell made no reply.

"Oho!" said Salvago, rubbing his hands. "Our soulful and dearly beloved comrade has broken training, has he ? And only ten days to go before the race. So considerate. Always the little gentleman, Alan is. Won't Horace be pleased! So will our friend the Welsh Wizard, who will presumably be asked to row. So will Oxford, who will be assured of a romp-over. Fun and games!"

"Hullo!" said Scorby, coming up moist and shining from his bath. "Alan disappeared?"

"Yes," said the cox, in a low voice, "but don't make a song and dance about it. There are probably half a dozen reporters flapping their ears in the front garden, and we don't want any publicity if we can help it. There may be some quite innocent explanation."

"Little guardian of our morals!" sneered Salvago. "Have you become a deputy President or something?"

Tom Scorby pondered the matter.

"Don't be more offensive than you can help, Selfridge's," he said. "Cox may be right. If you ask me, I should say the silly blighter has woken up late, sneaked into the bathroom for a hot bath, and gone to sleep there. The bathroom over there—" he waved a hand "—has been locked ever since we came in from the run. We've banged on the door, but nobody's answered."

"Golly!" exclaimed the cox, and dashed across to the coach's room.

"Well?" inquired Lampson, looking up. "Shut the door, cox. What about it? Evening clothes gone, I suppose?"

"No," said Gawsell softly. "As far as I know, every stitch of clothing he possesses is there—except the pyjamas he slept in last night."

The President gave a low whistle. "Gone sleepwalking, has he, and fallen into the river? This complicates matters."

Major Lampson snorted. "He'll be picked up at Basingstoke or some-where, suffering from complete loss of memory. Really, Robert, this is too thick. Here am I, an old soldier, broken in the wars, come home expecting to get a little peace and quietness doling out a few well-chosen words of advice to a Cambridge crew, and you let me in for this sort of thing! Strokes mooning about all over the countryside in their pyjamas!" He snuggled back into his bed, and drew the blanket about his chin. "I'm going back to sleep," he announced. "If, in the course of the next few days, you manage to get a 'varsity crew together guaranteed not to behave like hysterical schoolgirls, you can wake me up and tell me about it. Otherwise, leave me alone, please." He turned over on his side, and executed a well-simulated snore.

The cox looked from the coach to the President, and began, nervously: "Excuse me, sir, but I can't help thinking———"

Major Lampson heaved a sigh, and murmured: "Heaven help us! Now

18

we have a cox who can't help thinking! And he deliberately makes me feel a hundred years old by calling me 'sir.' Fire away, cox, but don't keep me awake longer than you can help. I'm losing my beauty sleep."

"Well, sir," began Gawsell, "—I mean, Robert, and—and Horace——"

"That's better," muttered the coach.

"——I couldn't help feeling," the cox went on, plucking up spirit, "that, since all Alan's clothes are there except his pyjamas, he must be somewhere quite close. What I mean is, if he had been wandering about Putney in his pyjamas, we should have heard about it by now. His picture has been in the papers so much lately that anybody, let alone the Putney policemen who see us every day, would know who he was at once. And besides . . ."

"Your logic appears convincing, cox," said the coach, opening his eyes. "And besides, what?"

"——And besides, one of the two bathrooms is locked, and nobody can get in."

Major Lampson sat up abruptly, all pretence of sleep abandoned.

"Bathroom locked!" he exclaimed. "You *are* a blithering little fool, cox! Why didn't you say so at once, instead of going into all this rigmarole about Alan sleep-walking on the Dover Road in his pyjamas!"

"Fainted in his bath!" cried the President.

"Of course!" said the coach, springing out of bed and pulling on a dressing-gown. "Cox, you're an idiot! Come on, Robert!"

The three men bolted from the room into the hall. Half the crew were still standing about, with puzzled or anxious expressions on their faces. Bonzo Kirkpatrick approached the President.

"I say, Robert," he began, "this bathroom has been locked all morning, and we can't——"

"We know all that," shouted Major Lampson. "Come on, you fellows! We must break the door in."

There was a rush at the door, which gave way with a loud splintering of wood. Torn from its hinges, the door fell inwards, and the President, Salvago, Owen Lloyd, and Tom Scorby were precipitated headlong into the bathroom. Kirkpatrick stumbled after them; and then the portly figure of the coach, the cox on his heels, picked its way in. The remainder of the crew, attracted by the uproar, formed a knot round the ruined doorway.

After the first-mad rush, the raiders picked themselves up and looked about them.

There was a sudden gasp of horror, from half a dozen throats.

The bath was three-quarters full of water. In it, very still, lay a grue-some pyjama-clad figure, the knees drawn up and the elbows back in an unnatural attitude, the face downwards and under water.

The first glance over, Horace Lampson pulled himself together. The stout, pink-faced figure in the silk dressing-gown abruptly ceased to be comic, and took on at once a commanding aspect.

"Clear out!" he barked, in a tone which brooked no questioning. "Robert, you stay. The rest of you, get out. Go and get dressed, and go down-stairs. Cox! Where's cox?"

"Here I am, sir," replied Gawsell, close at the coach's elbow.

The "sir" passed unnoticed.

"Go at once and ring up the doctor—our usual doctor, James Trunch. He lives in Disraeli Road, quite near. Tell him to come immediately. And then you'd better get hold of the nearest police station. And tell the other men to keep quiet, and on no account say anything to the reporters, if any of them come. I expect they'll gather like flies if they smell anything. Now, cut along."

The cox sped away on his errand.

"Now then, Robert," said the coach, when they were alone.

The two men, the young, sturdy one still clad in pyjamas and bare-footed, and the elderly, rotund and half-bald one in the flowered silk dress-ing-gown, gazed silently down at the horrible thing in the bath.

The elder man leaned forward and gingerly touched the nape of the doubled-up figure.

"Quite dead, I'm afraid," he said softly. "We can't do anything. Poor old Alan!"

The younger man sank down on a small stool, the only movable piece of furniture in the tiny bathroom, and buried his head in his hands. The coach touched him upon the shoulder.

"A beastly blow," he murmured. "I know he was a pal of yours. It's your first experience, of course, but I went through the war, and saw one after another of my dearest friends go out, so I know. And it's knocked your Boat Race into a cocked-hat. Well, I was President once, in the Dark Ages, so I know that, too."

The young man dropped his hands to his knees, and looked up.

"Are you *sure*, Horace?" he said. "Can't we—damn it, we can't leave him like that!" He waved an arm towards the nameless horror in the tub.

"The police won't like us if we shift things about," replied the elder man. "But we might have a look. Come on, old boy!" he added, briskly, in an endeavour to arouse the other from his morbid lethargy. "We might as well see what on earth has been going on."

Together they approached the body.

"Hullo!" said Lampson sharply. "What the dickens——! Why, the poor fellow's trussed up like a fowl! No wonder he was all doubled up in knots! Why didn't we see that before ?"

"Good Lord!" exclaimed Robert, carefully raising up the bent-over torso. "Why, he's strapped up like a—like a——"

"Like a fowl, as I said," pursued the coach. "Look here! A long strap passed round his arms—a luggage strap, or something of the sort, by the look of it—and a length of picture-wire wound round the front of the strap, and fastened round his knees! What in——"

Robert Tatersale pulled himself up, and leaned against the wall, a strange look in his eyes.

"Horace, I don't like this," he gasped. "Do you—do you think it's *murder?*"

The coach looked at him.

"Murder!" he replied. "Well, I don't know. That's for the police to decide. A rum sort of murder, if it is one, I must say. The door was locked. What about that?"

"There must be a key," muttered the young man.

"As you say, Robert, there must be a key," said Lampson. "A key to the door—a key to the mystery." He stepped across to the fallen door, and lifted it up.

"There is no bolt, but there is, or was, a lock. Hence, as you observe, there must be a key," he went on. "Aha!" He stooped, and picked something up.

"A key it is," he observed. "And it seems to be the right one." He stood up, and gazed round the small room. Apart from the door, its only aperture to the outside world was formed by a window, which gave upon the garden at the back of the house. He raised up the door, and inserted the key into the keyhole. It did not operate the lock, but, since the lock had been wrenched apart in the onslaught on the door, this was scarcely surprising. However, the key comfortably filled the keyhole, and, on being turned a few degrees, produced a half-hearted click from the interior of the wrecked lock. Lampson withdrew, satisfied.

"The right key, all right," he said. "Since it was lying on the floor underneath the door, I take it that it was knocked out when we broke the door down. And where is your murderer now?"

"That's all very well," answered Robert, a look of horror still in his eyes, "but how did he tie himself up like that?"

Major Lampson considered the body, lying still in the bath, its head fallen forward in the position in which it had been found.

"I have known stranger things," he said. "I won't say suicide, and I won't say accident——"

"Accident!" cried the young man. "How could it be accident?"

"You never know," said the other, philosophically. "Some silly idea of tying himself up to see if he could Maskelyne himself out of it again— some rag with some of the other men." He sighed. "I don't know, I don't know at all . . . I think, Robert," he went on, "we had better get out of this. We'll only make ourselves morbid, stopping up here. You'd better come downstairs and have some breakfast."

"Breakfast!" exclaimed the President. "Breakfast, with that——!"

"I'm sorry," said the coach at once, perceiving that the younger man's nerves were overstrung. "You come along, and we'll have a cigarette, and a dollop of whisky."

"Cigarette — whisky — training!" murmured Robert, as they descended the stairs.

"Training!" said the coach, turning to him with sudden asperity. "Don't be a triple brass-bound fool. What the dickens are you in training for, with *that* upstairs?"

CHAPTER FOUR

Major Lampson and Dr. Trunch sat together in the little sitting-room downstairs. Dr. Trunch was an amiable, elderly man, of some fifty years. He had rowed in the first May Boat of a minor college many years ago, and, being resident on the spot in Putney, had constituted himself physician in ordinary to every succeeding Cambridge crew. He had never been eminent as an oarsman, and he was no more than a general practitioner of ordinary merits; yet he was liked by crew after crew, and by their coaches, because he never pretended to be more than the garrulous hail-fellow-well-met that he was.

"Dreadful affair!" said the doctor.

Major Lampson pulled at his cigar. "I've three separate grey patches that I didn't have last night," he said. "Look here. You're a doctor, you've seen the body. What the devil do you make of it?"

The doctor pondered.

"Well," he said, finally, "the poor fellow was drowned."

"We all know that," said the other impatiently.

"He was drowned because he was lying face downwards in a bath of water, with his arms and knees all tied up like a parcel."

"Could he have done it himself?"

"Um!" said the doctor. "That's a difficult question. If you mean, had he the mental urge towards tying himself up like that and drowning himself, I should say no. Yes, considering what I know of him, what I remember from my last chat with him, only yesterday at lunch, I should say no. Highly strung, yes. But not the sort of fellow to do a fool thing like that, no."

"That's not what I meant, Trunch," said the coach. "I'm just as good a judge of psychology as you. If I weren't, I shouldn't be coaching this boat. I mean no offence, of course."

The doctor made a deprecatory movement.

"What I mean is," the coach went on, "could he have done it himself? Physically, not psychologically."

"Well, I think so," replied Trunch. "I can't tell you till I've tried, what? But I see no reason why, for reasons of his own, he should not have trussed himself up, and dumped himself face downwards into the bath."

"By Jove!" cried the coach, starting up. "I didn't think of it—but if he had chucked himself into the bath, he would have made the dickens of a splash, wouldn't he?"

"Of course."

"Well," Lampson continued, *"did he?* I'm blessed if I can remember, although I damwell ought to. Because, if there was no splash, he was laid in the bath by somebody else, and that's murder!"

The doctor shut his eyes for a moment, to the exasperation of the excited coach.

"Yes," he said, at length. "I remember now. There *were* splashes on the floor, and on the wall next the bath. So that's all right."

"Oh," said the coach, disappointed. He sat back, and took up his cigar once more.

"Can you think of anything else?" he inquired. "Anything about the body, apart from the attitude and the trussing-up?"

"Only the bash on the head," replied Trunch.

"Bash on the head!" exclaimed the coach, sitting up again. "Hang it, man, don't keep springing these things on me! He wasn't bashed on the head, was he?"

"But of course," said the doctor, calmly. "Had you only looked, there was a distinct abrasion on the left temple. It must have been a strongish knock, but the skin was scarcely broken, and there was very little blood. I don't blame you for not seeing it."

"Left temple!" murmured Lampson. "Full marks to you, and a bad one to me for missing it. He was lying with his head forward, as you know, facing the taps, with the wall on the left-hand side. So, as we didn't want to manhandle him—the body—too much, on account of the police, we missed that. But what was it? A blow from some weapon?"

The doctor smiled. "Now you're asking," he answered. "How the dickens do you expect me to know how it happened? I can only tell you that he hit his head, or something hit his head, on the left-hand side. But please don't ask me how. I'm not a diviner."

He paused. A thumping noise, as of the trampling of elephants, broke the stillness of the house.

"Your friends, the police," he said, smiling. "On the job, and they mean you to know it."

Outside the door voices were suddenly raised. The quiet but clear voice of Jelks, the butler, was first heard.

"Mr. Tatersale is the President, sir," it said. "I have already exceeded my duty in allowing you to see Mr. Tatersale, and——"

"Hang Mr. Tatersale, and you too," said a fresh voice, explosively. "I don't want to see an infant in arms! There must be some boss of this show—some respectable, grown-up man! Come, my lad, come!"

"Mr. Tatersale is the President, and in sole control here."

"Then heaven help Cambridge!" cried the voice. "I've seen your Mr. Tatersale, and he's about as helpful as a dying duck in a thunderstorm. Haven't you got a coach, or a dean, or a proctor, or something?"

Major Lampson rose, and flung open the door. "Can I be of any assistance?" he started to say.

Suddenly his eyes opened wide, as his gaze fell on the slim, dark-haired man in the bowler hat and blue serge suit who was cross-questioning the terrified Jelks in the passage outside.

"MacNair!" he cried.

"Good Lord! Horace Lampson! You here!" was the no less eager reply.

The two men wrung each other warmly by the hand.

"Gosh!" said MacNair. "So you're running this home of mystery and terror, are you? Yes, now I remember, you were an Oxford and Cambridge Old Blue, or something, weren't you?"

"My word!" said the coach. "I last saw you at Armentieres, just before you temporary blighters went home to be demobbed. You *were* tiddly that evening—but what are you doing here, and now?"

"What am I doing?" said MacNair. "Do you ask? You rang up hectically for the police, and the local Roberts, hearing that somebody in the Cambridge crew had been scuppered, had a fit of cold feet and asked for assistance at once, and I was sent here—and now you have the almighty-cheek to ask what I am doing here! Verily, the man hasn't changed one bit."

Lampson looked at the other.

"Do you mean to say you're the police?" he asked.

"Police?"echoed MacNair, indignantly. "Listen to the man! Am I the police! Laddie," he went on, tapping Lampson on the chest, "I am more than the police. I am Scotland Yard."

Lampson sank into a chair.

"Let me digest this," he murmured. "So much has happened this morning that I don't know where I am. Do you mean to say that you, Angus MacNair, the legendary Half-Wit of Flanders, are from Scotland Yard?"

"Strange, but true," said MacNair.

"My hat!" exclaimed Lampson. "But—but nobody asked for Scotland Yard."

"You didn't, Lampers," replied MacNair, "but, as I have just been try-ing to tell you, the local people quickly realised, very sensibly, that there would be the hell's own uproar, in the press and elsewhere, as soon as it was known that there had been hanky-panky amid one of the 'varsity crews, so they sent for us at once. Hence me. Hence my myrmidons all over the place. Of course," he went on, standing over Lampson and wagging a forefinger at him, "I haven't looked into this matter, and you, chum of my boyhood, may for all I know have all sorts of ber-loody mysteries to conceal. Hence your agitation on seeing me, said he in his best Sherlock Holmes manner."

Major Lampson pulled himself together. "I'm sorry," he said, "but this affair has knocked me all endways. You see, I was looking after these lads. I don't suppose the Boat Race means much to you—I don't mean to be personal, of course, but you see what I mean—no more than a Cup Final or a Wimbledon tennis tournament—but it means the dickens and all to some of us, and a thing like this——" Unable to complete the sentence, he motioned expressively.

The other's manner changed at once.

"I'm a fool, Lampers," he said, softly. "I know I've got a rotten habit of playing the buffoon. But, in a beastly job like mine, you've got to take things pretty lightly or you'd be in Dottyville in a month. . . . Do you feel up to showing me—the ropes? I wouldn't ask, only your butler seems to be all over dithers, and I couldn't get much out of your President, or whatever you call him."

"Certainly," said Lampson, rising. "I'll take you upstairs. But honestly, I don't know why the Yard should have been called in."

"New Scotland Yard, if you please," said MacNair. "Only novelists say 'the Yard.' "

"Have it your own way," was the reply. "But really, it's a clear case of suicide. No spectacular arrests for you, Angus." One hand, slightly tremu-lous, on the banisters, he climbed the stairs. "But the police will be the police. I suppose Sir Francis Woodgate will be turning up any moment."

"Well," answered the detective, "as a matter of fact he will."

The coach groaned. "Of course you would ask him. Reams of public-ity. Screaming headlines in the gutter press—the very last thing we want."

"Make your mind easy on that point," said MacNair. "If there's one job the much-maligned police are good for, it's keeping reporters at bay. Not a word of information will appear that hasn't been edited by me. I've got two men at the gates specially to keep 'em off."

Major Lampson grunted. "So *you* say. But if they can't get facts they'll go home and write columns and columns of the most loathsome bilge, full of vamped-up interviews and 'sensational disclosures,' plastering us with every scrap of mud they can rake up from the sewers of Fleet Street."

"Not if I know it," MacNair replied soothingly. "We have our methods. I've put the fear of God into reporters before now, old boy, and, by the living Harry, I'll do it again! Especially when a pal of mine like you is in it! . . . Come on, now, where's the *locus criminis*?"

They had by now reached the head of the stairs. Lampson silently pointed to the wrecked door of the bathroom, by the side of which a burly uniformed constable stood on guard.

"Hmm!" mused the detective, pausing before the wreckage. "How did the door get smashed?"

Major Lampson explained. "When we heard that Alan was missing, and that this bathroom had been locked for some time, we broke down the door."

"I see. Do you mind giving me complete details as to time, people you had information from, and so forth? This is where the note-book appears." He produced a leather-bound note-book and a pencil. "Some people think," he continued, "that only low-grade traffic cops use these aids to memory, and that real detectives ought to sniff about, look wise, and pack everything away in the little grey cells. An error, my boy. Disabuse your mind of it. Not being Lord Peter Wimsey, but a common or garden Robert, I have to write things down. . . . Now, then. You've made me chatter so that I forget the names. At seven forty-five Jelks woke you, and brought you a cup of tea and the newspapers. Jelks is our friend the dithering butler? Thank you. At about seven-fifty the crew returned from their run, and the cox (Hugh Gawsell—thanks) told you that stroke was missing. The President. . . . Yes, I've got that. At eight-five, or thereabouts, you, and cox, and the President, and others, broke the door down. The others were . . .?"

Lampson answered, to the best of his ability.

"And in what order did you enter the bathroom?" pursued MacNair. "You can't remember? Well, very likely it doesn't matter. The door was locked, not bolted, on the inside?"

"There is no bolt."

"I see. I should imagine, looking at the debris, that the top hinge gave way first, then the lock, then the bottom hinge. . . . Um . . . You say the key was found underneath the door?"

27

"It was."

"Good. Now," said the detective, "can you remember this: did you hear the key fall to the floor just before the door gave way?"

The coach pondered for a second, then replied: "I don't think so, but I really can't say. In any case, the crashing of the woodwork made such a row that I don't think I could have heard the key fall."

"I see," replied MacNair. "Well, that just about finishes the door. Finger-prints—hopeless. The whole blessed crew must have shoved against it. . . . Now for the bathroom itself. Nobody been inside who oughtn't to have, I suppose, constable?"

The policeman drew himself up. "No, sir, I was stationed here at eight thirty-five, sir," he intoned, in the expressionless voice peculiar to the constabulary, "and since then no person, authorised or hunauthorised, has attempted to enter the room."

"Capital!" exclaimed the detective. "That's something, although we are still left with some fifteen minutes in which anybody may have come in and done all sorts of monkey-tricks."

"I hardly think so," said Lampson, seriously. "Robert—that's the President—and I stayed here for perhaps ten minutes, after clearing out the others. . . ."

"Alone?"

Lampson looked at him angrily. "Yes, alone, Mr. Policeman," he replied. "Alone. And if you think we cooked up any evidence together, you can say so, and clap on the darbies at once."

MacNair laughed. "Don't be a fool, Lampers. Just the born inquisitiveness of a policeman. Besides, I don't carry darbies, as you so melodramatically call them, about with me. I find they spoil the set of my clothes, so I let my subordinates carry them. Much simpler."

"All right," said Lampson, mollified. "Anyway, after we left the room the other members of the crew were continually dodging about outside, since all their bedrooms, or nearly all, are on this landing, so that nobody could have got into the bathroom without instantly being noticed by the others."

"I see," replied MacNair. "Well, let's go in." He stood for a moment at the door. "Nice linoleum," he went on, "but footprints out of the question. Herds of muddy-hoofed elephants trampling all over the place."

"They had only just come in from their morning run, you see," said Lampson, "and it's wet underfoot outside, so the people who broke in made tracks all over the floor, I'm afraid."

"They would, of course." The detective strode over the broken down door into the bathroom. Confronted with the gruesome figure in the bath, he halted, and thrust his hands into his pockets.

"A nice little problem for a March morning," he muttered. "Has—has this been moved at all?"

"Robert and I lifted him—it—up a bit," replied the coach; "but when we saw that he was past help, we let—it—down again in the position in which we found it."

"You didn't attempt to undo these straps?"

"Of course not."

MacNair seated himself on the small stool, and contemplated the body.

"A nice go!" he murmured. "If this was his own bright idea as a new and original kind of suicide, well . . . Well, I wish he'd confined himself to the good old cleaning-a-revolver accident. If he was trying to be funny, and it was an accident—Well, I shall be very, ve-ry annoyed. If somebody else did it—if, I say—then, by glory, if I don't gather him in I'll kick myself from here to Old Bailey. And I'll let you help me."

"Do you mean, help you to solve this business ?" asked Lampson, with interest.

"I meant, help me to kick myself," said the detective. Observing the other's fallen countenance he went on, "but of course I shall want your help, since you will have to tell me all about everybody, and the events that led up to this. And, since you're a pal of mine, we can talk things over in a friendly way. There won't be any third-degree stuff—as far as I'm concerned."

"Thanks," said Lampson. "Do you want me to tell you what I can now?"

"Not just yet. At present I know nothing, and that's just what I want. I only know of this young man that he was a member of the Cambridge crew. I don't know anything about him, or about any of the other people in this house—no, not even you, really. I mean, in relation to this problem. I want to see the mere physical puzzle as a problem *in vacuo,* for a moment."

He gazed slowly about the room.

"Accident—suicide—murder," he murmured. "Body trussed up with a strap and some wire, and lying face downwards in a bath half-full of water. Slight blow on the temple—might have been caused by falling against the side of the bath, might not."

"Can you tell whether he could have done it himself? It beats me, and it beats Trunch."

"Who's Trunch?" asked the detective sharply.

"The doctor—our own doctor—who came first thing and saw the body."

"I see. Well, in answer to your question, it beats me, too. The body will have to be photographed, and the experts will have to make their report before we can say anything definite. . . . Now let's get on. Splashes of water on the wall and on the floor. Footprints and finger-prints all over. Hopeless to try to get anything from them. Now, what else have we?"

He rose, and walked across to the wash-basin.

"Nothing much here," he observed. "Cake of soap—a common coal-tar make—dry except for a wet, greasy patch on the underside. A nail-brush, quite dry. A sponge, pretty dry. A bath-towel, dampish. Do you know anything about any of these?"

Lampson inspected them. "I generally use this bathroom," he replied, "as it's nearest my room. I've always seen the soap and the nail-brush there, but I don't think the sponge is a regular fixture."

"Hmm," said the other. "I don't suppose there's anything in it, but we might be able to find out where it came from. Well, that finishes the wash-basin. What next? Ah, the window."

The window was of large size for a bathroom; the bottom half was glazed with opaque glass. It was almost fully open at the top.

"Was the window like this when you first came in?" asked MacNair.

"Yes," was the reply. "It generally is."

"Odd," commented the detective. "I keep mine tight shut at this time of year, but you athletes are queer folk. Let's look at it. Just big enough for a slender man to get through, but he'd leave traces."

He pulled the stool to the window, and was about to mount on it, when he halted abruptly, murmuring: "Careless, careless!" He bent over the stool and carefully examined its surface.

"A few scratches," he remarked. "Somebody *has* been standing on it."

In turn the coach bent with interest over the stool. "Does it give you any clues?" he inquired.

"None in particular. It has probably been stood on fairly recently, but I can't say more."

"Oh," said Lampson, in a tone of disappointment. "I should have thought you would have measured the marks, to see if they fitted anybody's shoes, and examined the scratches with a glass, to discover dust particles and things."

The detective laughed. "I'm not Thorndyke," he replied. "We aren't issued with pocket vacuum-cleaners like his. Those scratches are much too faint, and don't prove anything. Having seen that they were there, I shall now proceed to make some more."

Clambering on the stool, he examined the open aperture of the window.

"No marks here," he said. "The top of the window-frame is pretty grimy, and it would show up finger-marks like anything. No scratches on the paint, as far as I can see. I think any entrance or exit by the window is ruled out. Is this your garden it looks out on?"

"Yes," replied Lampson.

"I must have a look at the ground under this window," said MacNair, stepping to the floor. "Well," he went on, "for the moment that settles this room, I think. We must see what the experts say about the body; then I must look at the ground under the window, and try to trace that sponge, and of course the strap and the wire. Then, I mean to have a careful look at that door again, and see if there could have been any possibility of turning the key from the outside."

"Good Lord!" exclaimed Lampson. "Do you think——?"

"No, I don't," was the reply. "At present, I merely observe. Now, I know there was something else on my mind. . . . Of course!" MacNair cried suddenly. "What was I thinking of? The light! It's turned off. Was it like that when you came in?"

The other's face dropped suddenly. "I am an ass!" he faltered. "I know you'll never forgive me, MacNair. The light was on when we broke down the door, but, as it was broad daylight, I automatically switched it off, without thinking."

The detective looked at him gravely. "You *have* made a ruddy hash, and no mistake," he said. "Even Watson would have known better. It's hard enough to get prints on a small object like an electric-light switch, and now there'll be nothing but yours."

"I'm awfully sorry," said Lampson, in contrition. "I did think I had been careful to leave everything as we found it."

"Never mind, Lampers," said the detective, putting a hand on his shoulder. "It can't be helped, and I dare say it won't make any difference. Now, show me this boy's bedroom."

Major Lampson led the way. The room had not been entered since Gawsell left it, and it remained as he had described it to the coach. MacNair made a careful scrutiny, and, having satisfied himself, left the room, followed by Lampson.

"Don't let any one in that room, or in the bathroom," said the detective to the constable on duty. "On second thoughts, I don't think we had better allow any one on this floor. Where are the crew, by the way?" he inquired, turning to Lampson.

"They're all in the billiard-room at the back, I think," the coach answered. "They're keeping away from the front of the house, on account of the people outside."

"They can stay there for a bit, I expect," said MacNair. "I shall want to see them all, separately. Is there some other sitting-room I can use?"

"Certainly. I'll show you." Lampson led the way downstairs.

As they reached the foot, there was a ring at the front door.

"Reporters, I suppose," Lampson growled. A constable cautiously opened the door, and parleyed for a moment before admitting a group of men.

"Splendid!" exclaimed MacNair, rushing forward. "Here's Sir Francis and the photographers and all. Now we can get on."

As the detective greeted the new arrivals, and proceeded to converse with them in low tones, Lampson turned and entered the billiard-room.

CHAPTER FIVE

The crew were assembled in the room; some listlessly turning over the pages of books or newspapers, some, hands in pockets, staring out of the windows into the garden. The billiard table stood swathed in its cover.

"Anything new?" asked the President, looking up eagerly as Lampson entered the room.

"Nothing much," replied the coach, sinking into a chair and lighting a cigarette. "I've had a long talk with the police inspector, who turned out to be an old pal of mine. We went over the bathroom and the bedroom pretty carefully, but if he picked up any clues he didn't tell me."

"He—he *is* dead, I suppose?" inquired Ramsey, nervously.

"I'm afraid so."

There was silence for a few minutes, broken by Westlake, who threw down his paper with an angry gesture.

"I can't read these beastly papers," he exclaimed. " 'A good day's work by Cambridge—a record broken.' 'The excellent judgment shown by the stroke was mainly instrumental in——' Bah! It's too ghastly!" He rose from his seat and paced to the window.

"Cheer up," said Salvago grimly. "Think what the evening papers will be like. Boat Race tragedy! 'Orrible details!"

"Shut up, can't you," snapped Westlake.

"Yes, shut up, Selfridge's," said Robert Tatersale. "We can do without that sort of thing." He turned to the coach. "What have you in mind for our programme, in view of all this?" he asked in a low voice.

Lampson meditatively puffed at his cigarette before replying.

"It's beastly difficult to say," he answered. "It depends rather on what the police say. We shall hear from them presently, when they have decided whether it was accident, suicide, or—what. Even if it's just some silly accident, there can be no question of a race on the eighteenth. That, of course, is certain."

The President nodded agreement.

"I expect Tony Bellison"—this was the Oxford President—"will come round shortly," Lampson continued. "You and I, and Lewis, and the Oxford people must talk it over. It will be a nasty jar for them, but of course they wouldn't dream of insisting on a race."

"Do you think we might make some agreement to send both crews to Henley, for the Grand?"

"Perhaps," said the coach. "There would be a bit of sickness in some of the colleges; they would say we were spoiling the Mays and the Eights. . . . But we can only wait and see. We don't know what circumstances may arise."

"Then I suppose there's no need for us to stay here much longer, with nothing to do," said Tatersale.

"None at all," Lampson replied emphatically. "We obviously can't do any rowing, and you fellows could hardly put your noses outside the door without being goggled at by a mob of ghouls. We had better break up the practice immediately, and I should think everybody, except perhaps you and I, ought to be able to get away by to-morrow." He extended his cigarette case to the other. "Have a cigarette. You had several earlier this morning, but this will be symbolic."

There were stares from the crew as the President struck a match and exhaled a cloud of delicate smoke.

"Hullo," exclaimed Scorby. "Training over?"

"Yes," said the President curtly. "Did you think we were going down to the river to row a course this morning?" He proceeded to outline the decision that had been reached.

"But—but, do we clear out of here immediately?" asked one puzzled oarsman.

"To-morrow, probably."

"And I should advise you all," added the coach, "to get right away from London as quickly as you can. Go to the Continent for a bit if you can manage it, or some quiet place in the country. If you don't you'll be badgered to death by the newspapers for the next week or two. Personally, I shall get Lewis to take me to Scotland, and let him teach me golf."

There was a general murmur of talk among the crew.

"My luck!" muttered Salvage "I get into the boat at last, and then it's all washed out because a nervous, over-strung fool——"

"Easy, easy," said Kirkpatrick, in a soft voice. "It hits me, not to speak of Harry and Jack, just as much as you. And we don't know what happened yet. It may have been an accident."

"Of course it was an accident," interposed Jack Ramsey warmly. "Alan was an odd chap, but I've known him longer than most of you, and he would never have gone off the deep end like that. To be quite frank about it, I don't think he had the guts."

"There's a third possibility," murmured Hugh Gawsell, from behind a newspaper.

"What?" asked Ramsey.

"Murder."

Scorby looked at him with an angry frown. "Good Lord," he growled, "what an ass you are, cox. You've got murder on the brain. You worried us all last night with your bone-yard ideas, when nothing had happened; you might at least shut up about it now."

Horace Lampson's quick ear had caught some of the above dialogue from the opposite end of the room, where he was still in conversation with the President; and he now broke in angrily.

"Who's that talking about murder? Cox, try not to be more of a blazing little idiot than God made you." Addressing the crew generally, he went on: "Look here, you fellows. I know this business is hard on you, particularly on the new men, but we must put up with it. Try not to talk about it too much—and, above all, don't let any silly rumours get about. If a reporter asks you anything, keep your mouths shut. If he persists, dot him one on the jaw."

At this moment there was a sound of many footsteps on the stairs, and a murmur of voices in the hall. The front door was heard to slam; then the face of Inspector MacNair appeared at the door of the billiard-room. The crew, who had been confined to the room since the arrival of the police, looked up, curious to see what Scotland Yard might be like in the flesh.

"Sir Francis and the rest have gone," said MacNair, addressing himself to Lampson. "I shall want to see everybody who was in the house last night. I shall start with the servants. Can somebody come and act as a messenger for me, to dig out the various people as I want them?"

"Cox, that's your job," said Lampson. "Run along." Gawsell sped with alacrity on his errand.

After a further twenty minutes had been spent in desultory conversation, the cox reappeared.

"Well?" asked several voices.

"What did the servants have to say?" inquired the President.

"I don't know," answered Gawsell. "I waited outside, in the hall."

"What? Didn't you listen at the keyhole?" said Salvago, affecting surprise. The cox disregarded the remark. "Old Jelks was in a rare dither," he said. "I don't know what he told the sleuth, but I imagine he deeply incriminated himself, and all of us into the bargain. Anyway, he wants to see all you blokes now, separately."

"Who, Jelks?"

"No, you ass. Hawkshaw the Detective. I've been through it."

"What's it like?" came a general chorus. "Third degree stuff? Did he kick you in the stomach, like they do in the films, and say 'Come clean, or I'll give you de woiks'?"

"You'll find out soon enough," replied the cox briefly. "Now then, who's next?"

"I've talked to the beggar already," said the President.

"Yes, he told me that. He doesn't want you again, just yet. Bonzo, what about you?"

"Not me," said that gentleman. "Give me time to think up an alibi."

"You might as well take it in order," interposed the coach. "Cox has been, so seven had better go next, then six, and so on. Seven, you're for it."

Leopold Salvago rose from his seat, and, swiftly controlling himself after a perceptible moment of unsteadiness, walked to the door, followed by the cox.

"A bit green about the gills," murmured Scorby, when the door had closed.

"So will you be," growled the President. "You're next, you know."

Some time later, when the spare man, the last to be interviewed, was undergoing his ordeal, a commotion was heard in the hall. Lampson, moving to the door and opening it, heard voices in altercation.

"Confound it all, constable," came a high and peevish voice. "I don't care if the Home Secretary himself says I can't go in. I don't care how many corpses you've got. I don't care if the place is an absolute shambles. I have a lawful right to enter this house, where I belong."

"Where you belong is outside," retorted a heavy voice. "And I don't care if you're the Crown Prince of China. We don't want your sort in here."

The policeman was about to shut the door by main force, when Lampson hurried forward.

"It's you, Lewis!" he ex+++claimed. "Just the man I want to see. It's all right, constable, I can vouch for this gentleman. He has every right to be here. Come in, Lewis!"

A thick, blue-clad arm barred the passage. "Excuse *me*," said the policeman. "It's not all right. My orders is that nobody comes in here without authority. No, sir," he added loudly, for the benefit of any official ears which might be listening, "it's no good your shoving 'arf-crowns at me. I know my duty."

About to expostulate further, Lampson changed his mind, and tapped at the door of the small sitting-room.

"Yes?" said MacNair sharply, appearing at the door. "Oh, it's you, Lampers. What is it?"

"This is Mr. Bethell, my colleague as coach," replied Lampson. "He has every right to be here, but your bull-dog won't let him in."

MacNair surveyed the newcomer. "If you vouch for him, I suppose it's all right," he said. "Yes, bring him in by all means. I shall want to see you directly, by the bye. I'll send Mr. Gawsell here to find you, shall I?"

The wrath of Cerberus appeased, Bethell entered.

"Horace, what on earth has happened?" he asked, his face lined with agitation. "I had a late breakfast, as I usually do, and just afterwards I heard boys in the street with mid-day papers, bawling some rigmarole about a Boat Race tragedy. There were only a few lines in the paper, something about Alan having been found dead. I hope that isn't true?"

"I'm afraid it is," was the reply.

"Good God!" exclaimed Bethell, deeply shocked. "But—how? I tried to get you on the telephone, but I couldn't get an answer."

"I fancy the police have taken our telephone under their wing."

"But why the dickens are the police here? Is it a police matter?"

"Come into the garden," said Lampson, taking him by the arm. "I'll tell you all about it."

A few minutes later the cox appeared, with a summons to Lampson from the detective. As the three re-entered the house, MacNair met them at the sitting-room door.

"There you are, Lampers," he exclaimed. He mooped his brow. "What a morning! I say, I hate taking possession of your house like this, and sending people to fetch you, and all that—but it's all in the game, you know. Can I have a word with you in here?"

"Do you mind if Bethell comes too?" Lampson asked. "He's really just as much in charge of the crew as I am, and I expect he can tell you a lot about them, although of course he wasn't here last night."

The detective assented cordially, and the three men, shutting the sitting-room door behind them, sank into chairs.

"You weren't here last night, then, Mr. Bethell?" asked MacNair.

"I must qualify that somewhat," replied the former. "I dined with the crew, as I usually do. They went upstairs to bed shortly before ten, and I sat in here with Horace, talking shop, until about half-past. Then I went home in my car."

"Home being where?" inquired MacNair. "You must forgive my asking these things, but it's a matter of routine."

"The Senior University Club. I always stay there when I am in town."

"I see. And was everybody in a good temper at dinner?"

"Yes, I think I can say they were. They had a glass or two of champagne—it was what we call a fizz night, a reward for their exertions on the river. To men in training a very little goes far, so there was general good-humour at the table, and a bit of mild horse-play with sofa-cushions and the like afterwards."

"How about Strayler? Was he as cheerful as the rest?"

Bethell pondered before replying.

"I should say that he was as cheerful as he ever is—was, I should have said. He was always a rather morose bird by nature, if I may say so."

"But he wasn't any more morose than usual at dinner? Did he seem to have anything on his mind?"

"Well," said Bethell, "I think Horace will agree with me when I say that he appeared his usual self."

"Yes," put in Lampson. "He certainly smiled now and again, and made one or two jokes, but he appeared a bit snappish when others cracked jokes against him. But he was always like that."

"And the others were all quite merry, you say?" asked the detective.

"I think so," replied Bethell. "But you mustn't put the word merry in inverted commas, you know. Robert Tatersale was pretty sedate, but I imagine he feels it his duty as President to set a good example. I can't think of anything else; can you, Horace?"

"No," said Lampson, meditatively. "Old Salvago was a bit inclined to make himself objectionable, in his usual manner, by coming out with elaborately sarcastic remarks."

"That's the foreign-looking chap, isn't it?" MacNair asked. "An odd sort of fish. I didn't know what to make of him."

"No more do we, sometimes," said Lampson. "We only put him in the boat a few weeks ago, and we occasionally wish we hadn't."

"Now, apart from last night, when everybody was naturally more or less cheerful," said MacNair, leaning forward, "have they as a general rule been good-tempered and happy?"

The two coaches looked at one another. Finally Bethell replied: "That's an awkward question. No crew in training, that has been rowing together for weeks on end, with practically no change of company, is ever really good-tempered. Rubbing up against each other all day long, with no escape, is apt to fray their nerves to some extent."

"Couldn't have put it better myself," said Lampson.

"Yes, Mr. Bethell," said the detective patiently. "But was this crew any better or worse in this respect than the average?"

Again the two coaches exchanged glances.

"Well," said Bethell, "I have seen worse cases. Haven't you, Horace?"

" Rather," replied Lampson. " I remember——"

The detective held up a hand. "Sorry to interrupt you, Lampers, but I want to get on with this job. Now, can you tell me what specific causes of friction there have been in this crew ? I know it's a nasty thing to have to ask, because it may seem to reflect on your capabilities as officers commanding this crew; but you must remember in the first place that I don't know a thing about rowing, or crews in training, so I must find out something about it all; and, in the second place, this may turn out to be a very serious matter indeed, and if it's to be straightened out personal feeling must go by the board."

"I quite understand," said Lampson. "Well, Lewis," he went on, "I don't know that we have any particularly grisly skeletons in our cupboard, but such as they are we'll trot them out."

"Capital," murmured the detective.

"All I can think of, off-hand," said Lampson, "is that there was a certain amount of ill-feeling when the crew was chosen. The usual silly sort of college rivalry, you know. I don't see what bearing this can possibly have on the matter, because it doesn't affect Alan Strayler at all."

"Never mind," said MacNair. "May I hear it, briefly?"

"Well," said Lampson slowly, "I don't see what all this has to do with the poor boy's death, but I'll tell you what I can. As I dare say you know, at both Universities there's always a fair amount of rivalry between the various college boat clubs, which isn't confined to the races, but spreads to such matters as the choice of the 'varsity crew, the control of the C.U.B.C., and so on. It's only natural."

"Just so," said MacNair. "By the way—excuse the pitiful ignorance of a flat-footed rozzer, but what is the C.U.B.C?"

"Cambridge University Boat Club," Lampson answered. "All it comes to in this case is that one of the colleges, which has been Head of the

River for the last couple of years, felt a bit pained about the election of the President a year ago, when Robert Tatersale got it—they reckoned that it should have gone to Tom Scorby, one of their own fellows—and I understand that they still have a grouse about the selection of the present crew. They expected to have more representatives."

"Most unreasonably," put in Bethell, "since they have two men in it, Scorby and Ramsey, while there is—was, rather—only one other man from the President's club, Alan himself."

"What are the names of these colleges?" asked MacNair.

Lampson accorded this information and proceeded: "That's not quite all, of course. Until a few weeks ago Lloyd, who is one of the Head of the River lot, was rowing seven, but we had to turf him out and put in Salvago, a member of the same college, though not the same boat club, as Robert and Alan. I believe Lloyd was extremely fed up about it, almost more so than is quite sportsmanlike, and I suppose his pals sympathise with him."

"He is spare man now, isn't he?"

"Yes."

"Is he the only one? I mean, in the event of a vacancy in the crew, would he have been a certainty for a place?"

"Virtually," replied Bethell. "We only have one resident spare man now, for reasons of economy. But one or two of the Trial Caps were warned to keep themselves available, in case of an epidemic of measles, or anything of that sort."

"I see," said the detective. "Now, were there any other causes of discontent or ill-feeling among the crew?"

Bethell sighed wearily. "As far as I know," he said, "the whole blessed lot were fed up with each other. But Horace, as the man on the spot, knows more about that than I do."

The detective looked inquiringly at Lampson.

"I'm afraid I don't know a great deal," said the latter. "They naturally keep their juicier bits of back-chat in control when I'm about. I rely on cox to report to me on the morale of the crew. I advise you to ask him."

"I've got quite a bit out of Mr. Gawsell already," replied MacNair, with a smile. "He seems an intelligent little shrimp."

"Intelligent!" groaned Bethell. "Good Lord! And he's as bad as the rest of them. Only yesterday he was being ticked off by both Alan and Robert, and feeling quite sore about it, too."

"Was he, now?" said MacNair. "That's interesting."

"Look here, Angus," said Lampson, looking curiously at the detective, "just what are you getting at? I'm hanged if I can see what all this stuff we have been talking about has to do with poor old Alan. Are you suggesting——"

MacNair held up his hand. "I'm not suggesting anything, old son," he said. "I'm trying to get a clear understanding of the whole affair. Personally, I don't think there is any deep mystery in it; but the Divisional Inspector has called in Scotland Yard, so Scotland Yard it has to be. I must earn my bread and butter, you know. . . . Now tell me what you can about Alan Strayler, and I'll go away."

Bethell looked at Lampson; Lampson looked at Bethell; and finally Lampson spoke.

"I think we must have given you a pretty good idea of his character, as far as we have been able to observe it. I never saw much of him except in the way of business—that is, rowing. I first saw him rowing in the Eton eight, two years ago, but I never met him until I had him in last year's 'varsity boat. He was never a very sociable fellow, and as far as I know nobody was really deeply attached to him. I suppose Ramsey, our only other Etonian, and Robert Tatersale knew him as intimately as anybody."

"What about his people?" asked MacNair. "Was he well-off?"

"I'm afraid I know very little about that," replied Lampson. "I understand his father is a widower, also rather of an invalid. I've certainly never seen him; I believe he keeps himself cooped up in the wilds of Yorkshire somewhere. As for money, I don't fancy there can be much. Certainly Alan never made any splash."

"Well, did he seem hard up? Any sign of money troubles at all?"

"I really haven't the faintest idea," said Lampson. "I shouldn't say that he was actually hard up, but of course I don't know. He never talked to me about anything except rowing."

"Nor to me," added Bethell. "In fact, he hardly ever talked to me at all."

"Women?"

"Good Lord, I don't know," said Lampson. "How should I know? He had a fair number of 'phone calls, and I suppose letters, but no more than any of the others. But there haven't been any women hanging about here, I can assure you."

"I see," said the detective, consulting his watch, and rising. "Thanks very much, both of you. I must be getting along now, but I expect I shall turn up again, like a bad penny."

"Look here," said Lampson, "why not stay to lunch? Provided that our domestic staff is in a fit state to give us anything."

"Sorry, Lampers," replied the detective with a smile, "I have to get back to Scotland Yard. All the big noises are going to have a conference on this case, and they would be all at sea without my invaluable assistance."

"I hope I may be forgiven if I am treading on forbidden ground," said Bethell as the three men moved towards the door, "but is it in order to ask whether you have formed any theory about this dreadful business?"

"I have the beginnings of one," replied MacNair. "But only a very little one—and it may curl up and perish before the cold blasts of fact from the experts' report."

"The true sleuth-hound touch," commented Lampson. "Nothing given away. By the bye, I meant to ask you—will it be all right for the crew to leave here tomorrow?"

"Not till after the inquest, I'm afraid," was the reply. "I know it will be pretty beastly for the young fellows to hang about here, but I'm afraid it's necessary. Alter the inquest, we shall see. The inquest will be held some time tomorrow."

Having taken leave of the two coaches, MacNair paused to give certain instructions to the detective-sergeant who was left in charge of the premises, and took his departure.

CHAPTER SIX

In the road outside the house a crowd was collected, in spite of the constant efforts of three uniformed constables to maintain free circulation. Patiently they stood and stared with intensity at the unresponsive front of the house; in MacNair's fancy, their eyes seemed to protrude in the bulbous fashion beloved of Mr. Bateman. Even the passengers on the buses craned eagerly for a glimpse of the house as they sped by. As the detective left the gate, the pop-eyes were abruptly swivelled in his direction. A dozen or so of the idlers surged towards him, but were held off by a stalwart officer while he made his escape. At the junction of Richmond Road, a few hundred yards down the hill, he picked up a taxi, and was soon speeding across the bridge towards Scotland Yard.

From the window of the taxi MacNair noted with interest the placards of the evening papers. "BOAT RACE TRAGEDY" announced one in black. "CAMBRIDGE CREW DEATH MYSTERY" proclaimed another, in red and black. " 'VARSITY STROKE FOUND DEAD" cried a third, in red, black and yellow. "DEAD 'BLUE' SENSATION," and "DEAD 'BLUE' LATEST" shrieked two more, in black and orange. He smiled grimly. It was not every day that Fleet Street could enjoy the ecstasy of telescoping two front-page affairs, such as the Boat Race and a mysterious death, into one super-sensation. The press, however, could have little real information to impart as yet, for MacNair had permitted only the barest communique to be issued:

Arrived at Scotland Yard, MacNair ascertained that the conference was not to take place until two o'clock. He repaired to his room, where, in the intervals of revising his notes, he partook of a light lunch. Presently he rose, collected his papers, and walked to a room in another part of the building.

Here was assembled a little group, comprising a C.I.D. Superintendent—a man whose name was well known to newspaper readers as one of the Big Four—Sir Francis Woodgate, the famous medico-legal expert, a secretary, and, surprisingly enough, a police constable who, apart from the uniform jacket thrown loosely over his shoulders, wore nothing but a singlet and drawers.

"Here you are," said the Superintendent, somewhat testily. "We were wondering where you had got to."

"Only just striking two, sir," replied MacNair.

"Well, never mind that. Now, I've heard what Sir Francis has to say about this ridiculous business. What have you to say?"

"I have my report here, sir," said MacNair, laying a sheaf of papers on the desk. "I was unable to find any evidence that any person other than the deceased was in the bathroom at the time of death. Leaving the body, which is Sir Francis's affair, aside, I found no evidence of a struggle. The door had been locked on the inside, and the key was found on the floor. The window was open at the top, but there were no marks or scratches to suggest that any one entered or left the room that way. Under the window there is a flower-bed, about two feet wide. It bore no marks, nor was there any evidence that the mould had recently been raked or smoothed over. Beyond the bed is a hard gravel path. The light in the room was burning when the door was broken down, but unfortunately Major Lampson, the coach, switched it off. The only articles in the room which were not part of its usual equipment were a nail-brush and a towel, both of which apparently belonged to the deceased."

"Why 'apparently'?" asked the Superintendent.

"The towels, bed-linen, and so forth," explained MacNair, "were not the property of the individual members of the crew, but belong to the owner of the house, so that all the towels are alike. The deceased had no towel or nail-brush in his own room, so I presume that they were his."

"Any signs of disturbance, or anything unusual, in the bedroom?"

"None at all, sir. The bed was slightly rumpled, but had evidently not been slept in. All his clothes seemed to be there; I went over the room with Major Lampson, who of course knows the sort of outfit these young fellows take with them to Putney, and he assured me that nothing seemed to be missing."

"Any papers?"

"There were none lying about. He had two locked suit-cases under the bed. I shook them, and there seemed to be very little inside, but I didn't attempt to open them."

"Hmm," mused the Superintendent. "It might be as well to search his effects, to see if you can find something that would indicate a motive. If this is a case of suicide, as I think it is, I call it damned inconsiderate not to leave a note of explanation, and not to make a tidier job of it. Did you discover anything that would point to suicide, or to any other solution?"

"I found no motive for suicide, sir," said MacNair, "but I won't say that the atmosphere was unpropitious."

"What on earth do you mean?" growled the Superintendent. "Talk plain English."

"Well, sir, the deceased, Alan Strayler, seems to have been a morose and nervy sort of boy. He was always grumbling, and quarrelling with the coaches and the other members of the crew. In fact, the whole blessed lot of them seem to have been in a nasty sort of temper."

"What was he quarrelling about, do you know?"

"Mainly about rowing, I fancy."

"Good heavens, man," the Superintendent exploded. "Young and physically fit men don't kill themselves just because they've had a row with a rowing-coach! I've read of a Dago who shot himself because he was left out of a football team, but Englishmen don't do that sort of thing."

"A normal man wouldn't," agreed MacNair, "but I'm not sure that this fellow was quite normal. By all accounts, he was a highly-strung and irritable boy, who might go off the rails for some reason that would appear trifling to other people. Besides, sir," he said learnedly, "crews in training, who have been seeing the same old faces for months on end, are liable to find their tempers worn very thin, and all sorts of odd things may happen."

"Seems pretty thin to me," said the Superintendent. "Depend on it, you'll find there's money trouble, or a woman, in it somewhere."

"I made inquiries about that, sir, but I couldn't discover anything."

"Well, what about his family ? Have they been seen?"

"As far as I know, sir, his only near relative is his father, who lives in Yorkshire."

"Has he been notified ? He ought to be able to get here for the inquest, and perhaps he can tell us something."

"The local police have been asked to get in touch with him, sir," MacNair answered.

"Good," said the Superintendent. "Now, what about the other people in the house?"

"I interrogated them all," said MacNair, "and I had a talk with the two coaches." He took up a paper from the desk. "I have my notes here, sir. Perhaps I had better read them?"

The Superintendent nodded assent, and MacNair began.

"I saw the servants first, sir," he said, "then the members of the crew in order. The cox acted as a messenger for me, and I was able to get quite a bit of information from him about the various people, which I supplemented later in my talk with the two coaches. In my notes I have put this information against each name, as well as my impressions gained from the interviews."

"I see," said the Superintendent. "Fire away."

William Jelks, butler," read MacNair. "An oldish man, extremely flustered, and scarcely able to give a coherent account of anything. Said the crew seemed in a normal mood when they went to bed. Noticed nothing particular about the deceased. Said he was 'always an odd young gentleman, with never a friendly word for anybody.' Sleeps at the top of the house, and heard nothing in the night. Called Gawsell, the cox, at seven-thirty in the usual way, and knew nothing of Strayler's death until he was told by Major Lampson.

"James Littlechild, manservant. A young man, hopelessly unintelligent. Went off duty after dinner, returned at half-past nine, before the crew had gone to bed, but did not see or hear them, as he went up by the back stairs. Sleeps next to Jelks. Heard nothing in the night.

"Mary Cooper, cook, and *Jane Parsons,* housemaid. Both left the house at eight-thirty last night, as they sleep out, and both arrived together at seven in the morning. They hardly ever saw anything of the crew, and knew nothing of the tragedy until informed by Jelks.

" *Thomas Henry,* chauffeur. Boards out. Went off duty after taking the crew up from the boat-house at four-thirty yesterday, and did not arrive until ten this morning. Could tell me nothing about the demeanour of Strayler or the others yesterday. They all appeared normal to him.

"That finishes the servants.

"Hugh Gawsell, coxswain of the crew. An intelligent young fellow, seemed eager to be of any help. Evidently a devourer of detective yarns. Told me he suspected that this was a case of murder."

"Hullo!" exclaimed the Superintendent sharply. "What made him say that?"

"I asked him," replied MacNair, "but he could only say that it looked that way to him. He had no suspicion of any particular person, but he told me that they had all been discussing murders before dinner last night, and that several of them, in a jocular way, had expressed a desire to murder somebody—the victims ranging from Strayler to himself."

"Rot," said the Superintendent. "Just grousing. Nothing in that."

"I told him so," said MacNair. "I told him that he would get himself into serious trouble if he went about repeating that sort of thing. However, he took himself very seriously, and told me that he was saying nothing to anybody but me. He said he had no wish to be a tale-bearer, that he would be extremely shocked if guilt were actually pinned to one of his crew-mates, but that 'in the interests of justice' he felt it his duty to tell me all he knew."

"Nasty-minded little brute," commented the Superintendent. "Go on."

"His story is as follows," continued MacNair. "Jelks called him at seven-thirty. He then, as was his duty, woke the other members of the crew, and the spare man.They were all in bed and asleep normally, but Strayler's room was empty, as I have told you. He spoke about the matter privately to Tatersale, the President, who told him to say nothing."

"Why?" interjected the Superintendent.

"Because they thought Strayler had merely gone off on some escapade. The crew went for their usual early-morning run, and, on returning to the house, Gawsell informed Major Lampson that Strayler was missing. It then transpired that one of the bathrooms was locked; the door was broken down, the first to enter being Tatersale, Salvago, Lloyd, and Scorby. The body was then discovered, and the room cleared at once of all but Major Lampson and Tatersale."

"Was there time for any of the others to remove anything, or do any sort of poodle-faking?"

"There may have been," replied MacNair, "but he would have had to be very sharp about it, I imagine.

"Well, that's all for Gawsell, except one thing. Lampson and Bethell, the two coaches, told me that he was himself rather sore against both Strayler and Tatersale, over some grievance or other. The next is Tatersale. I really saw him first, as a matter of fact." He turned to his papers once more.

"*Robert Tatersale,* President of the Boat Club, rows number five. His story of what happened in the morning agrees with Gawsell's. Said he had no idea why Strayler should do away with himself, except that he was highly-strung—as I have already told you, sir—He did not know Strayler very well personally; in fact, Strayler had no intimates. He knew nothing of any money or other worries Strayler may have had. Although he could tell me very little, his evidence was all quite straightforward. He seemed genuinely upset about the death.

"*Leopold Salvago,* rows number seven. Foreign in appearance and manner, though speaks English with no accent. Some sort of Anglo-Italian or Frenchman, probably. He had no new information to give me, but he appeared very agitated. Seemed to think I was going to arrest him on the spot, and volubly and quite unnecessarily professed innocence, and absence of ill-will towards the dead man. According to Gawsell, he felt greatly aggrieved against Strayler, Tatersale, the coaches, and in fact everybody in authority, because the boat was going badly, and the coach had pulled off some sort of faked-up record yesterday. Last night, he was the one who started the talk of murders. He is a Socialist—not that that proves anything, but Gawsell seems to think it does.

"*Thomas Scorby,* rows number six. Had nothing new to tell me. It appears that he was in the habit of constantly grousing against Strayler, and would scarcely speak to him." MacNair went on to explain the matter of inter-college rivalry, that he had learned from Lampson. "It was he who set Salvago off yesterday, by commenting on a detective novel he was reading.

"*Thomas Kirkpatrick,* rows number four. His bedroom is over the bathroom, and he fancies he heard water running last night. He is not sure of the time, as he was half-asleep, but puts it at past eleven o'clock. He paid no attention to it, fancying that it must be Major Lampson. He cannot remember hearing any voices. Gawsell tells me that, like almost everybody else, he was somewhat discontented. To me he appeared a good-natured, beefy, brainless type of young man.

"*Peter Lightfoot,* rows number three. Heard nothing in the night. According to Gawsell, he suggested, playfully, that some one of them should commit a murder, 'to make the newspapers happy.' "

"Whoever is responsible has certainly succeeded in that," said the Superintendent.

"*Henry Westlake,* rows number two. Had nothing fresh to tell me. Gawsell had no scandal to tell me about him.

"*John Ramsey,* rows bow. Shares a room with Kirkpatrick, but went to sleep directly, and heard nothing. He was at Eton with Strayler. His estimate of his character agreed with what I had gathered from the others. He told me, however, that he was convinced that Strayler was not the type that would commit suicide. I asked him whether, at school, Strayler had ever been known to practise conjuring tricks, tying himself up or anything of that kind. He assured me that nothing of the sort had ever happened. He was utterly at a loss to account for Strayler's death, but felt sure it must be an accident of some kind.

"*Owen Lloyd,* spare man. Was rowing in the crew for some time, but was replaced by Salvago; according to Gawsell and the coaches, he is still deeply resentful. When I spoke to him, he had nothing new to tell me. He did hot seem in the least grieved by Strayler's death; in fact he made no attempt to pretend that he was. He told me frankly that he had had an extreme antipathy for Strayler, but that he had no hand in his death. He said to me: 'Why should I be such a fool ? In ten days training would have been over, and I should have been rid of Mr. Ruddy Strayler.' I told him that he was doing no good to himself by talking like that, but he replied that it was not his habit to be a hypocrite; that he had nothing on his conscience, and had no fear in speaking his mind."

"Precious set of young ruffians!" observed the Superintendent. "Catch me sending a son to Cambridge!"

"*Major Horace Lampson,* the coach," read Mac-Nair, proceeding to give an abstract of what Lampson had told him that morning. "I happen to know him personally, sir," he added. "We were together through most of the war. I can vouch for him as an excellent fellow, absolutely straight in all his dealings. The last person on my list is Lewis Bethell, who is Lampson's colleague as coach. He left the house, after yarning with Lampson when the crew had gone to bed, at half-past ten, and didn't arrive this morning till long after I had got there. He was able to supplement a great deal of what Lampson told me."

"Well," said the Superintendent, when MacNair had finished, "a nice household, I must say. What do you make of it, eh, Sir Francis ?"

Sir Francis Woodgate, who had been an attentive listener during the Inspector's recital, looked at the two men and spoke.

"I applaud Mr. MacNair's thoroughness. Personally, I do not think that we shall be able to satisfy young Mr. Gawsell's expectations of a gory murder mystery; but perhaps it would be best to make no definite assertion until Mr. MacNair has seen the result of my few gleanings." He picked up a sheaf of photographs from the desk, and passed them to the Inspector, who studied them with interest.

"I first had the body photographed *in situ,*" continued Sir Francis. "I then had it carefully removed from the bath, and placed on the floor without disarranging the attitude. It was then photographed from three different angles. Here again," he said, pointing out certain of the prints to MacNair, "are photographs showing the arrangement of the strap and the wire in detail. Here is a close-up of the wound on the temple."

"By the way, MacNair," interrupted the Superintendent, "did you trace the strap and the wire?"

"I'm afraid not, sir," replied MacNair, somewhat abashed. "Sir Francis took them away with him."

"Mea culpa," smiled the expert. "I had to take them, in order to procure exact duplicates. In fact, here they are."

The Superintendent lifted the strap and the twisted length of wire from a table, and examined them closely.

"Looks like an ordinary luggage-strap," he said. "The sort of thing you fasten travelling rugs and so on with. I should say the wire is stout picture-wire."

"I then examined the body," Sir Francis went on. "The hands, of course, were tightly clenched. Unfortunately they were empty. In a novel, naturally the dead man would be clutching a button, or an incriminatory shred of cloth." He heaved a little sigh. " 'Tecs in the story-books have all the luck. However, undaunted, I went on with my survey. Death, I found, was caused by suffocation. I should say that he had been dead twelve hours when I saw him."

"That would put it at about eleven p.m., when Kirkpatrick heard the water running," said MacNair.

"Just so. The body bore no marks of a struggle, except for this very interesting blow on the left temple. There was very little blood shed, but a blow of that nature would be sufficient to stun momentarily a young man with a fairly thin skull like the deceased. As to what caused the blow, I cannot say. The head, as we found it, rested against the rim of the bath-tub, where the wound left a slight trace of blood."

"Could the wound have been caused by the body falling heavily against the side of the bath?" asked MacNair.

"Yes, I think so. It is, as you know, an old-fashioned bath, with a wooden rim, which forms a fairly sharp angle. A heavy fall against that would be sufficient to break the skin, and not leave a mere bruise, as would a smooth surface."

"Tell us about the trussing-up," said the Superintendent. "That's the important part."

"Aha!" said Sir Francis. "Now you shall see my little Houdini performance. I have the photographs here, and I procured duplicates of the strap and the wire, so that we can imitate our Parisian confreres and reconstruct the crime. The Superintendent has already seen it done, but we will repeat it for your benefit, Mr. MacNair."

MacNair looked at the expert in wonderment. Observing his puzzled gaze, Sir Francis laughed. "I can read your thoughts, Inspector," he said. "You are wondering, is this aldermanic old buffer going to tie himself up into knots like the Boneless Wonder?"

MacNair made polite noises of protest.

"He is going to do nothing of the kind, at his age," said Sir Francis. "We have a substitute here." He pointed to the constable, who had been waiting patiently in his scanty costume, and now came forward, casting aside his jacket.

"You're not a professional contortionist, are you, constable?" asked the Superintendent. "You did it with suspicious ease the last time."

"No, sir," replied the constable, grinning.

"Of course he isn't," said Sir Francis, with indignation. "I had him specially chosen, as a man of the same build as the deceased, and I particularly asked for one who had no experience in gymnastic cantrips." He handed the man the duplicate strap and wire. "Now then, Maskelyne, show us your paces."

MacNair watched keen-eyed as the constable twisted one end of the wire round the middle of the long strap, then, crouching down, deftly passed the latter round his body, outside the arms, and made it fast, with the buckle on the left side where his cramped right arm could most easily manipulate it. He then manœuvred the free end of the wire between his legs, and slowly bound himself in incredible coils.

Sir Francis, photographs in hand, stood over him, watching closely. "No—no—bring that end round *there*. . . . That's right. Now round the knees. . . . That's it. . . . Can you twist that last bit round so? Use your teeth, man, if your thumbs won't reach it. . . . Capital!"

He stood back and surveyed the trussed figure with a gleam of satisfaction.

"How's that, umpire?" he asked, looking round at the two C.I.D. men.

"Very pretty. Very pretty indeed," said MacNair, examining the result critically. "But did he do all that under water ? Or did he tie himself up first, then take a high-dive into the bath?"

"I fancy he sat, partly on the broad, wooden ledge of the bath, partly on the stool. Then he simply fell, or rolled in. Where was the stool when the body was found?"

"I don't know," replied MacNair. "I wasn't there, you see. It may have been standing, or lying on its side, near the bath, but with all those people trampling in, I dare say somebody picked it up and put it to one side without thinking. However, there were scratches on the top of the stool. I thought at the time that somebody had been standing on it."

"There you are, then," said Sir Francis triumphantly.

The Superintendent was still gazing at the bound man. "Now can he undo himself?" he inquired.

"I can't say," replied the expert. "He didn't do it last time—but I don't see that it matters."

"I'll have a try, sir," said the now red-faced and panting constable gallantly. For a minute or two he struggled, with small success, until in pity Sir Francis stepped forward and swiftly undid the buckle of the leather strap. Shaking off his encumbrances, the perspiring constable rose to his feet, rubbing his limbs where the tight wire had left angry red marks.

"It doesn't matter two hoots whether he can undo himself or not," said Sir Francis. "The point is that he could do himself up. That will be all, constable. You have done nobly. The C.I.D. is eternally in your debt. When you retire from the Force, you can earn a fortune on the Halls. Now you had better go and clothe yourself—and I dare say your stern taskmasters will let you off, that you may suitably refresh yourself."

"Don't tantalise the man," said the Superintendent. "They shut at half-past two, and it's three now."

"Well, then, a nice cup of tea," said Sir Francis. The constable, with a grin, saluted and left the room.

"Now then," said the Superintendent. "What do you say, MacNair? You have seen that Strayler could have tied himself up without help, and pitched himself into the bath."

"Yes, sir," replied MacNair slowly. "I see all that. But I'm blessed if I can see him do it. What would be the point?"

"Don't be unreasonable, MacNair. You gave us long and convincing reasons just now why this young fellow, whom you describe as highly-strung and intolerably nervy, should have been capable of making away with himself."

"Quite so," said MacNair, "but why do it that way? Why not shoot himself?"

"Hang it, I said that an hour ago," said the Superintendent.

"Hadn't a gun," suggested Sir Francis.

"Well then," said MacNair, "if he was so keen on drowning himself, the Thames was quite handy. If he wanted to be really spectacular about it, he might even have leaped out of the boat in the middle of the race on Saturday week, and let himself be run down by the steamers. But why, why, why should any sane human being do such an extraordinary thing as to tie himself up in a parcel and suffocate to death in a beastly bath-tub?"

"He wasn't a sane human being," said Sir Francis.

"Well, I dare say he wasn't. But I don't think he was mad enough for all that silly performance."

"Accident, then," said the Superintendent. "Read about Houdini and these other people, and thought he'd try a little of it himself, by way of amusement."

"But why in the bathroom? Why not in the privacy of his bedroom ?"

"MacNair, you make me tired," said the Superintendent. "He went to the bathroom in order to try to escape from his bonds under water, just to make it harder. Then he slipped, hit his head, and was knocked unconscious just long enough to drown."

"I thought of that, sir," MacNair replied, "when I asked Ramsey if he had ever tried that sort of trick at school. And he never had."

"Oh Lord, oh Lord," sighed the Superintendent wearily. "I'm sick of this preposterous case. We should never have been called in. We have too much really important work to do, without this sort of thing. I've been worrying myself sick over that Wimbledon case for weeks, and now this crops up. If it isn't suicide it's accident, and frankly, who cares?"

"Don't say that, sir," said MacNair, somewhat shocked. "Now that I've been given this job, I want to get to the bottom of it. And, candidly, I'm not at all sure that it is suicide or accident."

"Murder, eh?" snarled the Superintendent. "You mustn't listen to that silly little fool of a cox. You have Sir Francis's opinion—you say suicide, eh, Sir Francis?"

"I do," said the latter.

"There you are," said the Superintendent. "Of course it's suicide. I confess I agree with you that the Maskelyne-and-Devant theory isn't as plausible as it might be. You go and get a suicide verdict at the inquest tomorrow. Unsound mind, of course."

"Very well, sir," said MacNair. "But if you don't mind, it would make me easier if I were to go back there, and make a few more inquiries."

"Have it your own way," said the Superintendent. "But don't bother me unless it's necessary."

MacNair was preparing to go, when the telephone bell sounded. The call was answered by the secretary.

"Hallo? . . . Yes. . . . Yes, he is here. Just a moment. Call for you from Putney, sir," he said, turning to MacNair. The Inspector went to the telephone. For a moment he listened, his eyes staring with amazement; then, shouting into the instrument: "All right—I'll be there immediately," he clashed the receiver on to its hook, and turned to the Superintendent.

"The D.D. Inspector at Putney," he said breathlessly. "He wants me to come at once. *He has found the weapon!*"

CHAPTER SEVEN

Jumping from his taxi, MacNair took the steep steps up to the front door three at a time. The constable on duty at the door directed him to the small sitting-room, where he found the Divisional Detective Inspector, who rose at once to greet him.

" 'Afternoon," said MacNair, plunging at once into business. "You've found——?"

"One of my men did, to be accurate, sir. The sergeant on duty at once notified me at the station, and I telephoned to you."

"Well—what is it?"

"This," said the Divisional Inspector. He pointed to an object that lay on the table, half enveloped in a large handkerchief. It was a spanner, made to fit a nut of about an inch in diameter, with a slender shank some five inches long, terminating in a wooden handle. MacNair picked it up gingerly by the shank, and peered closely at the head.

"Blood, I think," he said. "Hmm. . . . This changes the complexion of affairs. I hope nobody picked it up by the handle?" he added sharply.

The Divisional Inspector appeared deeply shocked. "Certainly not, sir," he said. "I hope we know better than that. It's been handled like a baby."

"Good," grunted MacNair. "We may get some finger-prints. In fact, the sooner we do that, the better. We'll send this off to Scotland Yard at once, before we do anything else. Can you lend me a plain-clothes man?"

"Certainly, sir."

"Thank you, Inspector—er——?"

"Jevons," replied the Divisional Inspector.

"Thank you," murmured MacNair, and sat down to write a hurried note, as Inspector Jevons left the room.

When he returned with a plain-clothes man, MacNair handed the latter the note and the spanner, carefully wrapped in the handkerchief.

"Hold this tightly by the middle, and by the middle only, as you value your life," he said. "I haven't any proper packing, and I can't wait. Take a taxi, go to Scotland Yard, and give this note to Mr. Simmonds. Tell him I want the prints on the handle of this spanner developed as quickly as possible, and good photographs made. You will wait until the photographs are ready, and bring them back here immediately. If there's any delay, raise hell. Don't be overawed by Scotland Yard. This is probably a case of murder."

"Yes, sir," said the man, opening his eyes wide at the last word.

"Now off you go. Tell the constable at the gate to get a taxi—don't attempt to push through that infernal crowd outside, or you'll spoil all our beautiful prints. . . . Now, Mr. Jevons," he added, as the man withdrew, "tell me all about this blunt instrument."

"The men were making a thorough examination of the grounds, as you ordered, sir," said Jevons, "when, less than an hour ago, one of them who was poking about, as it were, in a bush, found it, and at once reported it. That's really all. I'll show you the place, if you'd care to come out into the garden."

"By all means," said MacNair. Then, as they went down the steps at the back of the house: "Do any of the people in the house know about this?"

"I don't think so," replied Jevons. "It was kept quiet, and of course the 'phone message to you was from the station, not from here. But I won't say," he added, "that some of them may not have been looking out of the billiard-room window when it was found."

"Pity, that," mused MacNair. "I don't want a word of this to get about, not even to Major Lampson, until I know more. Now show me your bush—unobtrusively. We are in full sight of the house. Don't wave at it, I mean."

Inspector Jevons walked his Scotland Yard colleague a few paces further, then whispered: "That's the one. We passed it six yards back."

Smothering an exclamation of impatience, MacNair slowly turned, and made as if to pace back towards the house. Out of the corner of his eye he carefully scrutinised the bush and its position.

It was a fair-sized laurel, set against the seven-foot brick wall which divided the garden from that of the neighbouring house. From MacNair's position it partly masked a narrow passage between the party wall and the house, on the south, or uphill, side. Cautiously MacNair surveyed the building. A short flight of iron steps led to a narrow balcony. Behind this were the wide windows of the principal sitting-room, temporarily converted into a billiard-room during the tenancy of the crew. Within, MacNair could discern one or two of the oarsmen moving about. No one, as far as he could see, was watching the two detectives. On the floor above were five windows. From left to right, MacNair knew them to be those of a bathroom, the bedrooms of Tatersale, Salvago and

Strayler respectively, and another bathroom—*the* bathroom. Yet above were the bedroom windows of the second floor.

Taking his companion's arm, MacNair turned, and strolled slowly away from the house.

"Where, exactly, was the spanner found?" he asked. "Deep in, right on the ground, or what?"

"Pretty deep in," replied Jevons. "Impossible to see it if you weren't poking about with a stick, on the look-out for something, as my man was. It was where anybody might have chucked it, from the balcony or one of the windows."

"You think it was thrown down from the house?"

"Well, sir," said Jevons cautiously, "I won't say that whoever it was didn't just walk up and shove it in."

"Much safer," MacNair agreed. "It could have been thrown from the end of the balcony, or from the bathroom window, with fair certainty that it would go right in and bury itself. From anywhere else, it would be very risky. In fact, the only really safe way would be to shove it in, as you suggest."

"It beats me, though," said the other, "why, supposing this really is the instrument of a crime, it wasn't hidden better. Why leave the thing on the premises at all?"

"Of course," answered MacNair, "the whole thing may be a mare's-nest. It may be a simple case of suicide or accident, as we thought at first, and that spanner may have nothing at all to do with it. We shall know when we get a report about those finger-prints, if any, and the blood, if that's what it is. But if Strayler was really knocked on the head with it, I can answer your question about its presence in the bush. It was a poor hiding-place, but the only one available."

"But why not take it away with him?"

"Because he couldn't go away himself."

"Ah!" said Jevons. "An inside job, eh, sir?"

"Inside, if it's a job at all. Nobody broke into the house, that's certain. We should have his traces if he had. And, until I know more, I'm not going to entertain any theory of a mysterious outsider being let in by somebody inside—one of the servants, for instance. Whoever pitched his little life-preserver into the bush did it because he couldn't leave the house without exciting remark."

Inspector Jevons opened his eyes. "You don't mean one of the young gentlemen?" he asked.

"Why not? Even highly respectable gentlemen have been known to clock their pals on the head, or drill holes in them."

"Well, then, sir," said Jevons, "I dare say you're right enough about them not being able to get out of the house easily. They live under pretty strict discipline, as I know. They are hardly ever seen in the streets except to go down to the river, and half the time they make the trip in the car. And if they walk out without a cap they get cursed up and down, as though they were liable to die of pneumonia." He laughed. "And then they go down to the hard, put on practically nothing at all, and go rowing about for hours in the most perishing awful weather. Beats me what they do it for!"

"The policeman's lot is not the only unhappy one," smiled MacNair. "Anyway, I think we can say that the presence of the spanner in the laurelbush points to some one in the house, and probably not one of the servants, for they could nip out easily enough without attracting attention—not that I have any reason to suspect either the doddering Jelks or that half-wit Littlechild."

"And I forgot to mention," added Jevons, "that when they do go out—the crew, I mean—they can be spotted a mile off, in their woolly trousers and blue coats. They're about as inconspicuous as a torchlight procession with a brass band. You should hear the kids yelling after them: 'Good ole Kimebridge! Tike it orf!'"

"All the better for our job," said MacNair. "But all this is speculation. We haven't much to go on yet." He stared up at the house once more. "Yes," he mused, "the thing could have been pitched into the bush from the bathroom, by a man with a steady hand and a good eye. I wonder, though, would it have been possible for anyone to get out into the garden late at night, and shove it into the bush? You don't happen to know, do you?"

"No, sir. But I imagine it would be easy enough to get out through the glass door that leads on to the. balcony, then down into the garden."

"We must find out," said MacNair. "Meanwhile, I want to have another look at that bathroom. It was locked on the inside, remember."

The two men re-entered the house by the front door, avoiding the more direct passages through the billiard-room and the back door, and mounted to the first floor. The bathroom door, still guarded by a constable, lay in wreckage as it had in the morning.

MacNair and Jevons examined it thoughtfully; then, with the aid of the constable, raised it in position.

"No chance of the key being pushed under the door," observed MacNair. "It fits closely at the bottom. That, too, would practically prevent any light from shining under the door, which must have been useful to whoever was in here last night."

"I've heard of keys being turned from outside by means of a bit of string and a long metal skewer or what-not," said Jevons. "You pass the skewer through the ring of the key, tie one end of the string to it, pass the string under the door, shut it, and pull the string. The idea being that the skewer will act as a lever and turn the key, then fall to the floor when it has done its job, when you pull it out."

"I've heard of that, too," said MacNair, "—in story-books. I've never met it in real life, and I shouldn't much care to pin my chances on it if I were going to be a giddy murderer. Too risky. Still, we'll have a look at the key."

He stooped and picked up the key, which was still lying on the floor. "If there had been any monkeying of that sort," he said, as he scrutinised it, "your skewer would have left two marks on the ring—and there isn't a scratch." He examined the further end of the barrel. "No fancy work with pliers or forceps, either. We must think of another one."

"I remember reading a yarn," said Jevons hopefully, "where a man stuck a pin in the centre of a table and tied the end of a long thread to it. He passed the thread through a sort of grating in the door, then shut the door and locked it on the outside. Then he passed the thread through the ring of the key, pushed it through the grating, and let it slide down to the table. Then he hauled in his thread, and there he was."

"Very nice," said MacNair somewhat impatiently, "but there isn't a grating here."

"I know, sir," replied Jevons. "I put it forward as a case in point. Why shouldn't he have done the same thing here, only passed his thread through the open window, and slid the key down from the window above?"

"Feasible, I suppose," said MacNair. "I forget what window is just above this. Let's go and have a look."

The room overhead proved to be a small lavatory, adjoining the bedroom occupied by Hugh Gawsell. MacNair examined the tiny window with which it was equipped, and turned with a grunt to Inspector Jevons.

"It could be done, but it's another of these stunts I shouldn't attempt myself, if I were murdering somebody. It would go down well in print, but if I had a corpse down below in the bathroom I shouldn't waste any time in fooling about with pins and bits of string. These gadgets always go wrong at the critical moment."

"I'll tell you what, sir," said Jevons. "He went down to the garden to plant his spanner in the bush, then he went back on the balcony and threw the key in through the bathroom window from below."

MacNair pondered this. "Perhaps he did," he said, without enthusiasm. "Pretty clever of him. . . . Well, we'll leave it at that for the time being. Now that we are up here, let's have a look round."

Three bedrooms occupied the southern end of the house; the coxswain's tiny room, and two larger ones, one on the front of the house, one on the back. The former was shared by Westlake and Lightfoot, the latter by Ramsey and Kirkpatrick. Owing to the small size of the lavatory, part of the latter bedroom was directly over the bathroom, as Kirkpatrick had told MacNair. A rapid inspection of the three rooms revealed nothing to the detectives.

Opening a door covered with green baize, MacNair found himself in what was evidently the servants' quarters, reached by a separate staircase. Three small bedrooms were here. The first was empty; the second two were obviously tenanted, presumably by Jelks and Littlechild. A fourth door stood at the end of the passage. MacNair opened it, and discovered a small, dingy room, lit by a skylight, which apparently served as a box-room. Near the door stood a travelling trunk, of new-looking leather; further back, several other trunks of a heavy sort and a number of boxes and parcels, all thickly coated with dust, stood heaped; while, at the back of the room, two shelves held a confused mass of household debris and miscellaneous articles of no great apparent value.

Stooping, MacNair examined a luggage-label which was attached to the travelling trunk. "T. Scorby, Leander Club, Henley-on-Thames," he read. "This one evidently belongs to one of the crew. The rest of this stuff, I suppose, belongs to the owners of the house." Suddenly he straightened himself.

"I say, Jevons!" he exclaimed, "what about that strap? I'll bet it came from here. I brought the strap and the wire with me from Scotland Yard. Do you mind fetching them up, and also digging out old Jelks? I want a word with him."

Jevons, meanwhile, was rummaging among the shelves at the back of the box-room. "Certainly, sir," he replied. "I think I've found something here."

He turned, and exhibited in triumph a thick coil of wire.

"Good Lord!" cried MacNair, seizing it and carrying it to the light. "The very thing! The same stout picture-wire—and you can see, from the brightness of the metal, that a bit has been cut off here recently. Go and get Jelks at once!"

After what seemed an interminable wait, the old butler slowly puffed his way up the stairs, followed by Jevons, carrying the wire and the strap.

"Sorry, sir," said Jelks, apologetically. "I was having a bit of shut-eye in the pantry, not thinking I'd be wanted till tea."

"That's all right, Jelks," replied MacNair. "We want your valuable help for a minute or two. Have you got the strap, Jevons? Good. Now then, Jelks, can you tell us whether you have ever seen this before?"

The butler took the long leather strap, and examined it carefully.

"Why, yes, sir," he answered finally. "I have seen it. It doesn't belong to any of the crew. It belongs to the house. It's kept up here in this box-room, along with this other stuff."

"Good!" said MacNair. "Now, do you know anything about this coil of wire?"

Jelks looked at it. "No, sir. I can't say I do. I dare say it belongs to the house, but there's such a blasted lot of rubbish in here that I don't know all of it by heart. It isn't my job, not the things that belong to the house. I only noticed that strap there, because it was lying about when Littlechild and I took Mr. Scorby's trunk up."

"That's interesting," said MacNair. "Why does Mr. Scorby have a trunk up here?"

"Mr. Scorby's the Secretary," replied Jelks. "Trunks aren't allowed in the usual way, but the Secretary generally takes one because he has all the books and papers and things to cart about. The rest of them, they have to put up with suitcases. Otherwise, it would load up the bus too much, taking our things here from Henley. Then Mr. Scorby, he says his room's too small for a trunk, so he takes most of his things out, and has the trunk put up here."

"He can come up here any time, then, to get things out of his trunk?"

"Any time, sir. So can any of the gentlemen. If they want to keep things in the box-room, there's nothing to stop them."

"I see," said MacNair. "Thank you very much, Jelks. That will be all."

The butler turned to descend the stairs, but halted for a moment.

"Pardon my asking, sir," he said, "but have you caught him yet?"

"Caught who?"

"The murderer, sir."

"Who has been talking about murders?" asked MacNair testily.

"Why, nobody, sir," muttered Jelks. "Only I thought from what Mr. Gawsell said there was a murder."

"Jelks," said MacNair with earnestness, "you will do me a great favour by telling Mr. Gawsell to go and boil his head. There isn't any murder. If there is, I'll let you know."

"Very good, sir," said Jelks, chuckling as he plodded down the stairs.

"Young Mr. Gawsell is an infernal nuisance," said MacNair a moment later. "Now, then. We know where the strap and the wire came from, but that doesn't get us much forrader. It appears that anybody could come up here during the day, when Jelks and Littlechild are on duty downstairs, and sneak anything that took his fancy. Most discouraging. But let's hope the report on the spanner will tell us something."

"Yes, sir," said Jevons. "We ought to hear" about that soon now."

"Any moment," replied MacNair, "unless—" He was about to add a remark which, on second thoughts, he rejected as implying disparagement of his messenger, the Putney C.I.D. man. "—Unless the Scotland Yard people are being unduly slack," he amended. "Incidentally, we might profitably spend our time collecting some finger-prints, against the arrival of the photographs."

"Yes, sir," said Jevons slowly. "You know best —but, have we the right? No one is officially suspected of anything yet; and our instructions have always been, since that Grape Street business some years ago——"

"That will be all right, you'll find," interrupted MacNair. "There are more ways in heaven and earth of taking finger-prints than are dreamed of in the Judge's Rules. Come on."

They descended the stairs, and entered the small sitting-room, where MacNair instructed the constable on duty to send Mr. Gawsell to him at once.

When the little cox entered, MacNair motioned him to a seat, and stood over him in a magisterial attitude.

"Now then, Mr. Gawsell," he began. "I took you into my confidence to a degree which I can only call out of the ordinary, this morning. I now find that you have been prattling fond nothings about alleged murders in front of the servants. Is this the way you repay me?"

The cox looked up at him with apprehension. "I'm sorry, Inspector. Somebody—Salvago, I think—asked me a little while ago 'how my murder was going.' I replied with some joking remark, which I forget. I had no idea that old Jelks was flapping his ears in the vicinity, nor that he would take our *badinage* seriously."

MacNair looked at him solemnly. "Do you consider this a time for what you are pleased to call *badinage?*" he asked, in the most awful voice he could manage.

"It shall not occur again," said the cox, humbly.

"Very well," said MacNair. He produced a small piece of paper, which he held out by one corner. "Now, Mr. Gawsell, I want you to look at this paper. Have you ever seen it before?"

Gawsell examined it, but made no attempt to take it.

"Yes," he replied.

The Inspector appeared to be somewhat disconcerted by this answer.

"You're sure you have seen it? Where?"

"In your note-book," replied Gawsell, breaking into a broad grin. "I know that one. Still, to oblige you, Inspector, I'll make my mark, and come quiet." Taking the piece of paper gingerly by a corner, he laid it flat on the table and carefully impressed the thumb and fingers of his right hand upon it.

"There," he said. "I'm sorry my fingers aren't greasier, but I hope that'll do. Now shall I send the others in for the same treatment?"

"No, you little devil," said MacNair, smiling in spite of himself. "Get out. And if you breathe a word about finger-prints to anybody, I'll skin you alive."

When the door closed MacNair turned to Jevons, who had been an amused spectator of the scene.

"A wash-out, I'm afraid. Still, I wasn't planning to catch all of them with that old wheeze. We must try another line. Come upstairs again."

MacNair instructed the constable in the hall to confine the members of the crew to the lower floor until further notice, then mounted to the bedroom, followed by Jevons.

The constable on duty outside the bathroom, who had seated himself on the stairs close by, sprang to his feet as the two Inspectors approached.

"I think the bathroom can take care of itself now, constable," said MacNair. "We have seen all we want of it—and the body has been laid in the bedroom, and the door locked, hasn't it? Good. Now then, I shall want your services for a bit. First of all, I want a tray. A large tray, of any sort. Get one from the pantry, and come back here."

"A tray? What for?" asked the mystified Jevons, as the man departed on his errand.

"Wait and see," said MacNair.

Presently, when the man had returned with a large tin tray, MacNair entered the first bedroom on the front of the house, that of Owen Lloyd. Crossing to the wash-stand, he wrapped his handkerchief about his forefinger and thumb, and carefully lifted the carafe and its attendant glass and placed them on the tray. Tearing a strip of paper from his note-book, he wrote the name "Lloyd" upon it, and deposited it in the glass.

"Capital things, tooth-glasses and so on," he remarked to Jevons. "Take prints like anything, and nobody ever cleans them much. We'll have a few prints of whatever servant looks after these things—we'll disentangle them later—and lots of Mr. Lloyd's. Simplicity itself."

The same procedure was followed in each of the bedrooms, and at last the two detectives descended to the sitting-room, followed by the constable, stepping delicately with his load of tinkling glassware.

"Now," said MacNair, "we can get to work. I suppose you have a photographer and a man who knows how to take finger-prints?"

"Certainly, sir," replied Jevons. "I can telephone to the station, and they will be here directly."

"No, no! Don't telephone from here. Send somebody. I can't very well send all this stuff to Scotland Yard, and I want it done quickly."

An hour later MacNair, with a cup of tea by his side, sat contemplating the photographs which had arrived from Scotland Yard. Presently he tossed them over to Jevons.

"Lovely prints!" he said. "Couldn't be clearer. And the bloodstains *were* bloodstains. This is going to be real fun and games. I don't set up to be a finger-print expert myself, but I wonder. . . . Let's have a look at those glasses."

He bent over the tray of carafes and glasses. On each of them numerous finger-prints now stood out boldly designed in white powder.

"Hmm!" he murmured. "I don't know, of course—I don't know—but it seems to me——"

A knock at the door interrupted him.

"Now we shall know!" he cried. "Here are the photographs of our crockery."

In a few moments, the new photographs were unpacked and spread out on the table, while the two detectives bent over them eagerly. Presently MacNair took one of the Scotland Yard photographs—one showing a clear impression of the finger-prints that had been found on the handle of the spanner—and silently placed it beside one of the photographs that had just arrived.

MacNair and Jevons looked at each other, and with one accord slowly whistled.

"By Jove!" said Inspector Jevons. "Who would have thought it?"

MacNair nodded. " 'All this shall to Lord Burleigh's ear,' " he said.

"Lord Burghley?" inquired Jevons. "The running chap? What's he got to do with it?"

"Not he, not he, my child," was the reply. "A quotation. Sheridan. I mean, I must pop off to see my revered superiors at once. And the inquest to-morrow! Then, then, Jevons, my old university chum, comes the tug of war!"

CHAPTER EIGHT

It had been decided not to hold the inquest in the house on Putney Hill. The house was still the only sanctuary of the crew, and it was thought undesirable to throw it open to a herd of jurymen and reporters—who would expect to be conducted upstairs that they might see the fatal bathroom for themselves—to say nothing of such members of the general public as might secure the privilege of admission. The "Oxford and Cambridge Arms," a new super-public-house in the High Street, was therefore chosen as the scene.

Early the following morning Sir Francis Wood-gate descended from a taxi and entered the public-house. A constable directed him to a small snuggery, where MacNair, a pipe gripped between his teeth, sat bent over a mass of papers.

When they had exchanged greetings, Sir Francis drew up a chair.

"The case has changed since I saw you last," he said. "I heard all about it last night. May I congratulate you?"

"I'd sooner you didn't just yet, Sir Francis," MacNair replied. "But thanks all the same."

"But it seems a clear case. You're going for a murder verdict, I suppose?"

MacNair pushed his papers aside, and leaned back in his seat.

"I want 'persons unknown.' You see, Sir Francis, apart from the finger-prints I haven't a shred of evidence. For one thing, there's no motive. You heard my report yesterday, and you will agree there's absolutely nothing to go on. And I haven't been able to find anything further since then. I don't want to make an arrest until I know more, much more, about Strayler and about the finger-print merchant."

"Surely the finger-prints themselves are convincing enough?"

"They look pretty damning," admitted MacNair, "but you couldn't build up a case for the Crown on them alone, with no sort of motive to show. Any clever counsel for the defence could knock the whole case into a cocked hat. No motive! The finger-print system isn't infallible! Even if they are the prisoner's paw-marks, what evidence is there that the blessed spanner had anything to do with the death? Add to that the inevitably tremendous popular sympathy with the prisoner, and where are you?

"No," he went on, puffing at his pipe, "I don't want an arrest, not just yet. I want to watch the fellow—he can't run away, and I can pull him in quick enough if he does—and build up a case first."

"Well," said Sir Francis, "that seems sound enough. I take it you have coached the Coroner, and that the finger-prints won't be mentioned this morning?"

MacNair's face clouded. "That's just the devil of it," he said. "I explained the whole matter to him, but he won't see reason. He's a fussy old fool, with a bee in his bonnet about laying cards on the table, being open and above-board, and so forth, and he seems to entertain a profound dislike of Scotland Yard and all its works. You find Coroners like that sometimes, you know. At first, I wanted the spanner business to be kept dark for a bit, but he wouldn't hear of it. When I saw how the land lay, I wasn't going to say a word about finger-prints, but unfortunately Jevons—the D.D.I., and, I'm afraid, a bit of an ass though well-meaning—Jevons let the cat out of the bag. Now this wretched Coroner is probably going to insist on the production of the photographs, but if I can possibly stop him I will. This is going to be an infernally delicate case, and I don't want my hand forced at the very start."

Sir Francis expressed his sympathy. "My evidence won't bother you, at any rate," he said. "I have no official knowledge of any spanners or finger-prints."

A few minutes later, when the inquest was due to begin, MacNair and Sir Francis made their way upstairs to the "banqueting hall," a long room decorated in a sham Tudor style, with a profusion of imitation oak panelling and gaily painted coats of arms. A long table at one end of the room accommodated the Coroner, his clerk and the jury. Other tables were reserved for the police and the press. The witnesses, including the entire Cambridge crew, occupied a front row of chairs; behind them, a sensation-seeking public filled every available inch of space.

MacNair took a seat between Jevons and Sir Francis Woodgate, and glanced curiously at the oarsmen. They sat in a stolid row, motionless and expressionless as though they were being photographed. He scanned each face in turn, but could read nothing.

The buzz of conversation that pervaded the room ceased abruptly as the Coroner began to speak. He was a short man, with a long and fleshy face, an arched nose which served as perch for a pair of pince-nez, and scanty grey hair.

Having announced his intention of briefly outlining the case, he proceeded to do so at great length. They were there to inquire into a terrible tragedy—for what tragedy could be more poignant than the sudden cutting-short of a young man in the prime of his youth, a youth upon whom, until two short days ago, not only his friends, but countless men and women, all over England, nay, wherever the English tongue was spoken, were relying to lead his University to yet another victory over their ancient rivals in what was, undoubtedly, the most famous sporting contest in the world. The Boat Race was, indeed, a national institution, which brought out the finest traits of the English character . . . the sporting instincts of the British race . . . they in Putney were proud that, year by year, the cream of young manhood from the two old Universities made their district the venue for this contest. . . .

"If there's much more of this," MacNair whispered, turning to Sir Francis, "I shall leave the room until I'm called."

The expert smiled. "He ought to take on John Dumbbell's job in the *Sunday Examiner,*" he replied.

The Coroner was still going strong. Never before had the Boat Race been marred by such a dreadful event. . . . Whatever the jury might find as the cause of death, the sympathy of the court must go out, first to the family of this unfortunate boy, and then to these young men, his dearest friends and daily associates . . . great blow to them. . . .

Glancing up, MacNair fancied he caught, upon Gawsell's shrewd little face, the ghost of a wink directed towards his neighbour, Salvago.

At length the Coroner ceased from generalities, and gave an account of the finding of the body, and the other events of the previous morning. Noting that the Coroner said nothing as to the discoveries of the afternoon, MacNair gave a little sigh of relief, and sat back to hear Robert Tatersale make formal identification of the deceased. The Coroner explained that the father of the dead young man, his only surviving parent, lived a great distance away, and was unable to attend the inquest.

"Now; Mr. Tatersale," he asked, "in what spirits did the deceased seem, the day before the tragedy?"

"Pretty much the same as usual," replied Tatersale, speaking calmly and with complete self-possession. "He was never very lively in manner, or talkative. I should say he was just his usual self."

"Nothing out of the ordinary, nothing noticeable?"

"Nothing that I could see, sir."

"When you say that he was never very lively," pursued the Coroner, "do you suggest that he appeared weighed down by cares or apprehensions of any nature?"

"I don't think so. I think it was just his natural temperament."

"Do you know of any worries of a private sort he may have had?"

"No, sir. As I said, he never talked much, and I really knew very little about him."

"But surely, as President, and as fellow-oars-man, you must have known him intimately?"

"I really didn't, although I was in the crew with him last year as well as this. He was never very sociable in his life at Cambridge. Apart from rowing, I saw very little of him."

"So you know nothing of his personal affairs? Nothing of his home life?"

"No, sir. I think I met his father once or twice, but that is all."

"I see," said the Coroner. "Now, did he ever say or do anything to suggest that the idea of suicide might be in his mind?"

"Nothing in my hearing."

"Did he," the Coroner asked, speaking slowly, "did he ever exhibit signs of apprehension of personal violence from any quarter?"

There was a sensation among the spectators, instantly glared down by the Coroner.

"Never," was Tatersale's firm reply.

The President stood down, and the witness-box was successively occupied by the various members of the crew, the servants, and Major Lampson. Their evidence was familiar to MacNair, and he contented himself with watching with a keen eye the demeanour of the various witnesses. Jelks, the butler, waxed garrulous, and the Coroner had some difficulty in stemming the tide of his trivial outpourings. He had nothing to tell but, evidently with some idea of maintaining the prestige of Cambridge against these Londoners, sang the praises of Strayler, the President, the coaches, and all the members of the crew. The other servants were brief, and added nothing material to the evidence. Major Lampson told his story shortly and with soldierlike directness. He did not, MacNair was pleased to note, go into any details concerning the little dissensions and jealousies of the oarsmen under his charge. That, after all, was the affair of the police, and need not be dragged into publicity for the titillation of the newspaper-reading public. Time enough for that when the scene was shifted to the Old Bailey.

The crew, for the most part, gave their evidence briefly and stolidly. MacNair shrewdly guessed that they hated the whole affair, and, with an eye on the reporters' bench, were determined to give the newspapers as little material as possible for flaring headlines and sensational articles. Even Gawsell, the cox, returned monosyllabic answers to the Coroner's questions whenever possible, and breathed no word of his novel-bred and fantastic theories. A slight sensation occurred when John Ramsey was asked whether Strayler, when at Eton, had ever been known to practise conjuring tricks or escapes from bonds; but the answer was an uncompromising negative. Salvago alone showed signs of nervousness, and answered the Coroner's questions with Latin volubility and frequent gesticulation. MacNair cocked an eye at him, and murmured: "Don't sing out, my lad, until you're hurt."

Owen Lloyd, the spare man, gave his answers curtly, with a scowl upon his dark, Celtic features that seemed to express contempt for the Coroner, indifference as to the manner of Strayler's death, and complete boredom with the entire proceedings. This concluded the evidence of the inmates of the house; and now Dr. Trunch, and the police sergeant who had first appeared on the scene, told their stories briefly.

Inspector MacNair was the next witness to be called. With the experience of many similar scenes behind him, and with a professional economy of words, he recited the evidence which he had decided was sufficient for the occasion. He described his arrival at the house, his examination of the body of the deceased and of the bathroom in which it was found, as well as of the deceased's bedroom; and he had interrogated the various inmates of the house, all of whom had already given their evidence. Having completed his set statement, he turned to leave the witness-box, when the Coroner stopped him.

"One moment, Inspector, one moment please," said that functionary, in a sharp voice. "Have you no further evidence to give?"

MacNair cursed under his breath, and replied: "No, sir. At this stage, we do not wish to bring forward any further police evidence, apart from the expert medical evidence that will be given by Sir Francis Woodgate."

The Coroner peered owlishly at him over the top of his spectacles as though he were a strange new animal, and sniffed audibly. "Very well, Inspector. But I must warn you that I will not have this court treated in a cavalier fashion by the police, as so many Coroners' courts are. We are not to be intimidated by great names from Scotland Yard. We are here to learn the truth, sir, the truth. . . . I call upon Sir Francis Woodgate to give evidence."

There was a stir of interest as the famous expert took the oath; was this indeed he, this stout, jolly-faced man with the big moustache, so utterly unlike the popular notion of the hawk-eyed sleuth ? There was almost an audible murmur of disappointment, so different was the real from the ideal.

Sir Francis gave his evidence in workmanlike fashion, interlarded with anatomical terms which were Greek to the jury, although the Coroner sagely nodded his head at each point. The deceased had died from suffocation, due to immersion in water; a bruise existed on the left temple, which might have been caused by contact with the sharp rim of the bath—or by other means, such as a moderate blow with a hard instrument. The skull of the deceased was thin, and such a blow, how-ever caused, could have induced loss of consciousness for a very brief period. It had been ascertained by experiment that the bonds by which the deceased was found trussed could have been secured by himself, when living. There was no evidence that any second party had, violently or with the connivance of the deceased, taken any part in the trussing. It was impossible to say whether deceased had been placed in the bath, or had fallen into it, deliberately or otherwise.

When Sir Francis had left the witness-box, the Coroner cleared his throat. MacNair, suspecting what was about to come, muttered words which spoken aloud would certainly have constituted contempt of court.

"I have reason to believe," said the Coroner pompously, "that the police have in their possession further evidence which should be brought forward, but which they have not seen fit to adduce. I am aware that in cases of this kind the police frequently hush up, if I may use the expression, vital evidence, for purposes of their own, and endeavour to secure an adjournment of the inquest at an early stage of the proceedings. In my view, gentlemen, such a course can only have the effect of debasing the proceedings of the Coroner's inquest to the level of a mere farce—yes, a mere farce. It must be obvious to the meanest understanding that the finding of the jury must be stultified if the police are to be allowed to freely suppress important evidence at will. We are here, gentlemen, to inquire into the death, the sad death, of this unfortunate young man, and we must see the thing through. We must put all our cards on the table, if I may use a gaming metaphor—though no one holds gambling in greater detestation than I do. I will therefore take it upon myself to call Police-Constable Whitely."

"Why isn't this man in Parliament?" groaned MacNair. "It's his obvious home, and he'd do less harm there than here."

P.C. Whitely proved to be the constable who had discovered the spanner in the laurel bush, and with much gusto described the finding of that implement.

"Is this spanner put in evidence?" asked the Coroner, when he had done.

MacNair slowly rose. "I have it here, sir. It can be put in evidence if you wish."

"I certainly wish," replied the Coroner tartly. "Mustn't withhold important evidence."

Inspector Jevons, who had seen the spanner before MacNair, now entered the witness-box; and, before long, he revealed, under the Coroner's searching questions, that photographs had been taken of finger-prints on the spanner, and also that finger-prints of the various members of the crew had been secured.

MacNair thrust his hands deep into his trouser pockets, and leaned back in his seat. "This really is the limit!" he whispered to Sir Francis Woodgate. "And of course I'll get all the blame at Headquarters. The inquest should have been adjourned at the outset."

"Why are these photographs not put in evidence?" asked the Coroner, staring at MacNair, who promptly leaped to his feet.

"This is very irregular, sir," he said, with some heat. "We have not——"

"It is for me to judge," interrupted the Coroner, "what is regular and what is irregular in this court. I will have no insolence from you, sir, whatever you may have been accustomed to in other courts. I think I have a right to ask for those photographs."

With ill grace MacNair complied. The photographs were handed to the Coroner, and passed round the jury. MacNair, once more in the witness-box, declined to express any opinion concerning the prints, alleging that he did not pretend to be an expert in that branch of the detective science.

"Very well, Inspector," said the Coroner peevishly. "I have never been so crossed by the police in my life—never in my life. However, I know that Detective-Sergeant Simmonds of Scotland Yard, who has been referred to as the finger-print expert who developed the prints on this spanner, is in this court, and I propose to call him."

Amid breathless interest, Sergeant Simmonds entered the witness-box. He testified that he had received the spanner at Scotland Yard the previous afternoon, and had developed the finger-prints on it. He was then handed the two sets of photographs, which he examined closely.

"Now, Sergeant," said the Coroner, "you are a finger-print expert, are you not?"

"I have been employed in the finger-print department at Scotland Yard for the past six years, sir."

"Very well. Do you identify the finger-prints found on the spanner with those in any of the photographs of the prints found on the glasses and carafes?"

"Yes, sir. The prints on the spanner handle are those of a right hand, and they agree perfectly with the impressions of the fingers of a right hand in photograph number 3."

"You do not know whose prints they are?"

"No, sir. The photographs are only marked with numbers."

"Thank you, Sergeant. That will do," said the Coroner. "Now, Inspector MacNair, I must call you again."

Heaving a sigh, MacNair rose slowly, and once more entered the witness-box.

"Now, Inspector. You have heard Detective-Sergeant Simmonds's evidence. *In whose room did you find the glass which was photographed as number 3?*"

MacNair paused for a moment, and glanced round the packed room. Every eye was upon him. He moistened his lips, which were unaccountably dry, and replied:

"In Robert Tatersale's."

A gasp, of horror or astonishment, went round the room. MacNair looked in the direction of the man he had named. His face drained of colour, his eyes horribly staring, the President sat, motionless, in his chair. After one incredulous glance in his direction, his comrades had turned their eyes away, and now sat transfixed, many of them as white as himself.

For a few moments there was a terrible silence; then the Coroner spoke, in measured tones.

"Thank you, Inspector. There will be no further evidence, I think." Turning to the jury, he began his summing-up, proceeding slowly, horribly slowly, as it seemed. Step by step he once more outlined the case, and the various points in the evidence they had heard. A bruise had been found on the temple of the deceased, which might have been caused by falling against the edge of the bath, or might have been caused by a blow from an instrument. Such an instrument had been found in the bushes outside, where it could have been thrown from the bathroom window. This instrument bore traces of human blood, and carried on the handle finger-prints identical with those found on a glass tumbler in the bedroom of Robert Tatersale. The jury must remember that it was not proved that the prints on the tumbler were those of Tatersale. All that could be said was, that the prints on the spanner agreed with those on the tumbler found in Tatersale's room, and with no others. No evidence had been brought forward that any person had a motive to wish deceased out of the way. The medical evidence had shown that deceased could have trussed himself up in the manner in which he was found, and could have fallen into the bath through his own volition, or accidentally, as well as been placed in the bath by any second person. Before bringing in a verdict other than one of misadventure or one of suicide, the jury must satisfy themselves that a second person could have contrived to stun deceased, with the spanner or otherwise, and during the brief period of unconsciousness have trussed him up with the strap and the length of wire, and placed him in the bath, in such a manner that deceased would not have been able to cry out for assistance, and rouse the house. The jury must carefully consider the evidence of the spanner; the fact that it bore finger-prints at one end, and human blood at the other, did not prove of necessity that deceased had been struck with it. On the other hand, if the jury were satisfied that the spanner had been used to stun deceased prior to .his being trussed and suffocated, they must take into consideration the finger-prints found on the handle of the spanner, always remembering that the evidence was purely circumstantial, and that the evidence even of finger-prints was not infallible. The jury must remember that its verdict was not by any means final, and a verdict of wilful murder brought by them against any individual did not imply the condemnation of that individual, for that could not happen until he was brought to trial. If, however, they were satisfied that deceased had met his death through the wilful action of a certain person, it was their duty to bring in a verdict to that effect, in order that the police might immediately apprehend that person and bring him to justice if he were guilty. The jury, therefore, had the following alternatives to consider, viz., suicide, misadventure, murder by person or persons unknown, or murder by some specified person or persons. It was now for them decide.

The jury put their heads together for a moment, after which the foreman asked permission to retire. This was granted, and the jury filed out into an adjoining room that had been prepared for them.

Sir Francis Woodgate leaned over to MacNair. "Hard lines," he said. "But I've had years of experience of this sort of thing, and I've met Coroners like that before. Lord bless you, yes! You remember the beach murder at Bournford? Ah, before your time, I expect. That was just as bad as this—worse, in fact. But it came all right in the end, and so will this."

"Humph!" grunted MacNair.

"You've got the right fellow, you know," continued Sir Francis confidentially. "I thought it was accident at first—not suicide, because nobody would be fool enough to want to kill himself that way—but this inquest has changed my mind. Depend on it, this was a right little, tight little murder. I know you haven't got a motive, but you can find one easy enough if you rout about a bit. Whatever verdict they bring in, I should pull him in at once if I were you."

MacNair's reply was cut short by the re-entry of the jury. At once the buzz of conversation that had arisen ceased as though a sound-proof curtain had been lowered. Solemnly the Coroner inquired the verdict.

The foreman of the jury rose to his feet. A petty tradesman from a Putney back street, he realised that his supreme moment had come. The eyes of England were upon him, as they never had been before, and never would be again. He gazed slowly round the court, stroked his waxed ginger moustache, and let drop the words which would send the telegraph wires of a nation humming.

"We find that the deceased perished through wilful murder, caused by Robert Tatersale."

As the foreman, trembling with the excitement of his world-shattering announcement, dropped back into his seat, MacNair rose and pushed his way past the jurymen, heedless of the murmurs, rapidly rising to an uproar, of the spectators, heedless of the formula which was being mumbled by the Coroner. His objective was a young man in a brown tweed suit, who sat slumped back in his seat, staring ahead of him with glazed and unseeing eyes.

MacNair's hand dropped gently on his shoulder.

"Robert Tatersale, I arrest you for the murder of Alan Strayler. Anything that you say will be taken down and may be used in evidence against you."

CHAPTER NINE

The result of the inquest had thrown the London press into convulsions. The arrest of the Cambridge President for the murder of his stroke was one of the cataclysmic "stories" that fall into the lap of astounded journalists only once in a lifetime. MacNair had often idly speculated what the contents-bills would say were Larwood, for example, to take ten Australian wickets with ten successive balls, dismissing the side for no runs. Here was something even more spectacular; and one evening paper, knocked all of a heap with the news, issued a contents-bill bearing nothing but a huge red "!" One or two papers immediately prepared hysterical onslaughts on the whole university and public school system; another, which viewed all things through red spectacles, affected to see behind the crime the sinister hand of Bolshevism; one paper alone maintained that Tatersale had been falsely accused, and had sharp words to say about police imbecility; and, from every newspaper office, reporters were sent off on frantic pursuits after the life-stories of all concerned. An important Cabinet crisis became lost to sight in the universal uproar.

The house on Putney Hill was besieged by sightseers and newspapermen, and it was obviously impossible for the crew to live there any longer. MacNair, however, knowing that the crew once dismissed would immediately disperse to the most remote sanctuaries that could be found, besought Major Lampson to arrange their temporary removal to some nearby spot, where he could find them if necessary. Accordingly, the Ranelingham Club offered the crew its hospitality for the time being. Here, in its spacious and secluded grounds, not too far from Putney, they would be free from molestation.

In the afternoon MacNair once more made his way past the police cordon into the house, where Hugh Gawsell and Tom Scorby, the honorary-secretary and now acting-President, were arranging the removal of the crew's belongings. The other oarsmen were already at Ranelingham. In the sitting-room, MacNair found Major Lampson and Lewis Bethell.

"Well, Angus," said Lampson, looking up, "coming to gloat over your horrid work?" He waved the detective to a chair. "You have made a pretty job of it, and no mistake. What do you mean by arresting my President on such a ridiculous charge? And why did you keep all this finger-print stuff up your sleeve until the inquest, hey?"

MacNair declined the whisky that was offered to him, and lit his pipe. "I'm sorry about it, Lampers," he said, "awfully sorry for your sake. The verdict was none of my doing. You ask why I kept the finger-print evidence up my sleeve. Well, as a matter of fact, I intended to let it remain there some time longer, but the Coroner was too much for me. I didn't want a verdict against Tatersale at all. My policy was to have been one of 'wait and see.' "

"Humph!" grunted Bethell. "You wanted to keep the wretched boy on a string for a bit, all smiles outwardly, waiting for him to incriminate himself. 'Dilly duck, dilly duck, come and be—hanged.' "

"I suppose," said Lampson, "you have some more evidence tucked away, or you wouldn't have arrested him."

"I had to arrest him, I tell you. The verdict left me no choice in the matter. But, since I *have* arrested him, I have had to pursue further inquiries. Some sort of a case must be built up."

"But, damn it, man, if you don't believe he's guilty . . ." Lampson began explosively.

"I don't say I believe him guilty, and I don't say I believe him innocent," replied MacNair. "If I find good evidence that he's innocent, of course he will be released."

"Rot," said Lampson. "I know you Roberts. Once you've arrested somebody, you'll work yourselves blue in the face to get him convicted."

"That's not really true, you know," MacNair replied quietly. "We are no more willing to hang an innocent man than you are. But it makes us look silly if we have to admit that we have pinched the wrong man, and we don't like that. That's why I must keep hard at work on this case. If I let the case remain as it stands now, Tatersale would almost certainly be found not guilty, and the murder would remain unavenged. For by that time the trail would be too cold to be gone over again in search of another murderer."

"Then you are convinced it is a case of murder?" asked Bethell.

"I think so. How else account for the spanner?"

"It looks pretty bad, I admit," said Bethell, "but it may have some innocent explanation. Have you asked Robert about it?"

MacNair grinned. "Tatersale, old chap, as man to man, did you bash Strayler on the head with this?" he mimicked. "As a matter of fact, the subject was touched upon in a little tête-à-tête we had at the police station. And of course he said he had never seen it."

"Well, very likely he hadn't," said Lampson. "That doctor fella—Sir Francis what-not—said that accident or suicide were not ruled out, didn't he?"

"He did. And if either turns out to be the truth, I shall be as pleased as you. But if Tatersale never saw the spanner, how did his finger-prints get on it? Did he pick it up in the dark, or play blind man's buff with it, or what?"

"Well, he may have been fooling about with it quite innocently," said Lampson, "and now, with a rope round his neck, of course like a silly ass he won't admit it. What was the spanner like, by the way? I couldn't see it properly at the inquest this morning."

"Could you see it, Mr. Bethell?" MacNair inquired.

"Yes, I saw it quite well."

"Have you ever seen one like it before?"

"It looked to me exactly like a boatman's spanner, for tightening the nuts on riggers. You'll see lots of them about in any boat-house."

"Capital," said MacNair. "You have confirmed what I thought. I showed it to your boatman a little while ago, and that's what he said it was."

"That's interesting," observed Lampson. "Did he identify it as his?"

"He told me, somewhat cautiously, that he couldn't be certain. He said that there were so many tools about the place, both those he had brought with him and those belonging to the boat-house, that he couldn't keep track of them all. He was pretty certain, however, that it wasn't one of his own."

"Good old Willie!" said Bethell with a smile. "He's not giving anything away. Did you ask Dursfield, the permanent man at the boat-house?"

"Dursfield?" said MacNair. "Little man, with a wizened face and a bulging head? Yes, I spoke to him, all right. He looked at the spanner, and said it might have been his. Then I got him to look through his tools, and he finally decided that it must be his. He had three of them, all more or less alike, and Willie, your own man, had one."

"So somebody must have pinched it from the boat-house, and brought it up here," observed Lampson.

"Evidently."

"Odd sort of thing to do," said Bethell. "Why cart a thing like that up to the house, when he could have laid his hands on a dozen things up here that would have done just as well? There was nothing else missing from the boat-house, I suppose?"

"Neither of the boatmen spotted anything," answered MacNair. "But they have such heaps of stuff there. Hammers, chisels, rasps, wooden handles for tools of various sorts—like our own Exhibit A, the spanner—queer things they told me were riggers and stretchers and I don't know what, contraptions for measuring the height of tholepins . . ."

"Rigger-sills, you probably mean, not tholepins," Lampson interrupted.

"Same thing. What does it matter? I had no idea that looking after a row-boat was such a whole-time job."

"Row-boat!" exclaimed Bethell with a snort. "Call yourself an intelligent detective officer, and allude to such a superb piece of delicate cabinet-work as a modern racing eight as a *row-boat!* Do you think we paddle about in our shirt-sleeves on the Serpentine, or what?"

"And that's what we pay rates for," added Lampson. "But tell us, Angus, has all your sleuthing produced a reasonable theory yet?"

MacNair put down his pipe, and looked at the two coaches. "I'm being quite frank with you two," he said, "because I know it won't go any farther. Honestly, I have only the glimmerings of ideas so far."

"And what is the glimmering?"

"Well, Robert Tatersale sneaked this spanner, took it up to the house, and hid it. Then, on Wednesday night, when the others had gone to bed, he went to Strayler's room, and invented some pretext for a quiet talk with him. He suggested that Strayler should go to the bathroom and go through the motions of taking a bath."

"Why?" asked Lampson.

"For privacy, and to provide an excuse in case they were found together after lights-out."

Lampson nodded. "Possible, I suppose," he said reflectively. "They are not supposed to take hot baths at odd moments without asking me, but I should only have been mildly angry if I had caught him."

"Exactly," said MacNair. "Enter infuriated coach in dressing-gown. Finds stroke having an illicit bath, President yarning with him. Tableau. President explains that he heard water running, went to see what it was, found stroke, and took the opportunity to have a quiet chat with him about the prospects for the race. Exit coach, mollified. But anyway, there was no need for that. Strayler probably got into the bath, to be ready for such an emergency. That's why he took his towel with him. When he wasn't looking, Robert sloshed him gently on the side of the head, and, while he was momentarily stunned, held his head under water. George Joseph Smith all over again—only Smith,

I believe, pulled their legs up suddenly. Some say he mesmerised them. I don't think our Robert is capable of that refinement. Then, when Strayler was drowned or nearly drowned, he tied him up with the strap and the wire that he had previously concealed in the room."

"But what for?"

"To suggest suicide or accident, of course. And it nearly took everybody in. Then he either dropped the spanner out of window into the bushes, or else he crept downstairs and out into the garden, and planted it there. I'm not sure which. I don't know how he wangled the key, but he may have chucked it through the open window of the bathroom from below."

"Robert was a pretty good cricketer, as oarsmen go, I believe," remarked Bethell, "so he might have been able to do that."

"There you are, then," said MacNair, triumphantly.

Lampson slowly filled his pipe and lit it before speaking.

"It's all very well," he said between puffs, "for you to say 'there you are.' But where are we, exactly? You can't hang a man, you can't hold him in custody for an hour, on far-fetched theories like that. Where's your motive?"

"Well, that's the weakest point in my case. I haven't got much of a motive. Perhaps something will crop up later. I couldn't get anything out of Willie, as you call him, or Dursfield, this morning. But I found a sort of boy, who says he works at the boat-house as Dursfield's assistant. . . ."

"Hardstaff. I know him," interjected Lampson contemptuously. "Nasty pasty-faced little shrimp. He would say anything."

"He told me," MacNair continued, in no way put out, "that he was cleaning up about the place on Wednesday afternoon. Tatersale and Strayler were later in leaving the changing-rooms than the others, and Hardstaff said that he heard them quarrelling, as he thought. He couldn't hear what they said——"

"Not for want of trying, I'll bet," said Lampson parenthetically.

"——but their voices seemed angry. Then they came out of the changing-room together, and stopped talking directly they saw him. According to him, Robert was black and scowling, while Alan's face was white with anger."

"Rubbish!" exclaimed Lampson. "The little fool got all that stuff from the cinema. He probably invented the tale in the hope of seeing his name in the papers."

"I don't know," said MacNair. "We have to get at the truth from all sorts of witnesses, you know. And I think Hardstaff was telling the truth."

"Even if he was," said Lampson, "it proves nothing. Alan was a touchy fellow, as you know. Probably Robert spoke sharply to him about his rowing, and he resented it. There's no motive for murder there. If any, you might expect Alan to dot Robert one, and not the other way round."

"As I have told you, I don't yet say with certainty that Robert is a murderer. But, if he is, here is the beginning of a motive. Robert got fed up with Alan's rowing; he got some idea that he was spoiling the crew's chances of winning the race. The idea became an obsession with him, until on that one point he became unbalanced. Without realising the full implications of his act, he determined to put his enemy out of the way; and, with the ingenuity of a monomaniac, he devised this peculiarly complicated way of doing it."

"Very ingenious, Inspector," was Bethell's comment, "but I can't see Tatersale in the rôle of a monomaniac. Why, look at the man! A stolid, beefy fellow, without many ideas in his head apart from rowing. That type wouldn't go off the rails, not in a hundred years."

"Then what is your solution?" asked MacNair.

"Accident. That or suicide."

"Then what about the spanner?"

"Oh, bother your spanner!" cried Bethell testily.

Further discussion was interrupted by a knock at the door. The knocker, on being bidden to enter, revealed himself as Hugh Gawsell, who cocked an inquisitive eye at the detective as he sidled into the room.

"Well, cox," said Lampson, "all packed?"

"Very nearly, sir—Horace, I mean," the coxswain replied.

"Don't call me Sir Horace. I'm not knighted yet—we'll all deserve it, though, if ever we unravel this conundrum."

"Tom and I were wondering what to do about Alan's things," Gawsell continued. "His room is still locked."

"The room will have to stay as it is for a bit," said MacNair. "We shall leave a policeman in charge of the house, of course."

"You might have known that," observed Bethell sharply. "You *are* an ass, cox."

Gawsell was about to leave the room when MacNair stopped him.

"Have you any more bright ideas? If so, you might trot them out, for we're pretty short of them just at present," he said with a smile.

His face brightening, the little cox closed the door once more, and seated himself.

"I've been thinking things over," he said, "and I suddenly remembered a story I read a little while ago. A bloke murdered another bloke, and he left a revolver lying about with a third bloke's finger-prints on it. He got hold of this other chap's prints, photographed them, and made a die from them out of celluloid or something, which he used like a rubber stamp."

"Oh, shut up, you blithering idiot," groaned Lampson.

"I'm sorry," said Gawsell, correcting himself. "It wasn't a revolver, it was a window-pane. And there was camel's blood mixed up with it some how, but I forget just how. But why shouldn't somebody have stamped Robert's finger-prints on that spanner, to cast suspicion on him?"

"Because nobody in this house had any celluloid or engraver's tools or camel's blood," answered Bethell. "Can't you think of anything more sensible?"

"The camel's blood had nothing to do with it really," protested the coxswain plaintively.

"Then why mention it?" snapped Bethell. "Talk sense, or clear out. How were the crew when you left them at Ranelingham?"

"Pretty grumpy, most of them. Salvago nearly bit a reporter's ear off when he tried to interview him, and then I rather think he went off to his bedroom to weep. Old Bonzo wouldn't talk to anybody, and he was pretty rude to the secretary at Ranelingham, although the chap was being as nice as he could. Lloyd put everybody's back up by making sarcastic remarks to the effect that *he* wasn't the only one to lose his Blue now."

"Do you know," Gawsell continued, leaning forward and speaking in a tone of mystery. "I think that bloke knows more than we think."

"What on earth do you mean?" asked Lampson.

"Well, he was very sore at losing his Blue. There's a motive. And he was talking about murders the other night. He was saying how simple it was to hit a man on the head on a dark night."

"You're a nasty-minded little beggar, cox," said Lampson. "That proves nothing. You'll be telling the police that I did it, next."

"I may be wrong," said the cox, wagging his head portentously. "But those Welshmen are crafty blighters."

MacNair leaned forward and tapped the coxswain on the knee. "Excuse me," he said, "but, speaking of talk about murders, didn't you, that same night, boast that with your medical knowledge you could overpower a bigger man than yourself, and cut him into little bits?"

"Who told you that?" asked Gawsell, growing pale.

" 'From information received,' " answered MacNair with a grin.

"Well," said the other defensively, "if I did say it, it was only because we were all talking about murders."

"Exactly," said Bethell. "What you said proves nothing, and what Lloyd or anybody else said proves nothing. If I were you, cox, I should put my head in a bag and boil it."

"Tell me, cox," said MacNair suddenly, "what was this story you read about the camel's blood and all that?"

"Something of Austin Freeman's, I think. I read it a few weeks ago, when we were at Henley."

"You read a lot of detective yarns, I suppose?"

"Yes, quite a few."

"And the rest of the crew read them too, do they?"

"Shockers are their sole form of literature," put in Bethell.

"I see," said MacNair. He mused for a moment, and then started on a fresh tack. "An ingenious idea of yours, cox, about forged finger-prints, but out of the question in this case. As Mr. Bethell so justly observed, nobody in this house could have carried on the business of an amateur die-stamper without attracting attention. Still, it was an odd thing to leave that spanner lying about, with its well-nigh damning finger-prints. Criminal carelessness, one might say."

"But he hid it in the bushes," Lampson objected.

"He did," said MacNair. "But I'm not so sure that he didn't want it to be found."

Lampson's pipe clattered to the floor as his mouth opened in astonishment.

"But—but what would he want to do that for?" he stammered. "Why should Robert leave his finger-prints all over this spanner, and then want us to find the infernal thing?"

Bethell smiled. "Calm youself, Horace," he said. "I see what our astute friend is driving at. It isn't a touch of the sun. You mean——" he turned to MacNair, "——you mean that *somebody else,* such as Lloyd, wanted us to find it?"

"Exactly."

"But it's absurd. I don't understand," protested Lampson.

"Never mind, Lampers old man," said MacNair. "You will some day. It's only an idea of mine. I may be quite wrong." He rose and moved towards the door. "Now I want to nose round a bit. Quite unofficially. You fellows can come, if you like. I may need your assistance."

Followed by the three others, MacNair crossed the passage, and halted at the door of the billiard-room.

"I don't think I have been in here yet," he remarked, "except to pop my head in once or twice. I didn't want to intrude on the crew yesterday. May I look in?"

"Rather," said Gawsell, opening the door. "You'll find the place crawling with clues, I dare say."

Tom Scorby, dishevelled and perspiring, looked up from his labours as the door opened.

"There you are, Guzzle," he said, eyeing the coxswain with disfavour. "I thought you were never coming back. You can't shirk your share of the Carter-Pattersoning, you know. I've left you all the books to pack." Catching sight of MacNair he continued, more politely:

"Good afternoon, Inspector. More cross-examination?"

"Not to-day," replied MacNair. "Just a little look round." He slowly surveyed the room. "Comfortable place. This was the crew's general sitting-room, I suppose?"

"Yes."

"All the home comforts, I see. Nice billiard-table, gramophone, piano, books, magazines. . . ."

"We may as well notify what's-their-names that they can take their billiard-table away now if they like," said Scorby. "I'll write to them. The piano belongs here."

He crossed the room and lifted a pile of sheet music from the top of the instrument.

"Most of this belongs to Alan, by the way," he went on. "Do you want to impound it as evidence, or what shall we do with it?"

MacNair glanced at the music, and laid it down. "Leave it there for the moment. It will be put with his other things, which will all eventually be turned over to his family. Anything else of his here?"

Scorby turned to a shelf, which supported a disorderly array of books.

"Some of these may be his. I don't know who they all belong to. I was going to take them all to Ranelingham—or rather, cox was."

MacNair, joined by Bethell and Lampson, examined the row of books with interest.

"A curious assortment," mused the detective, fingering one or two volumes. *"Bantu Dialects— Pitt and the Great War*—thought he was dead then—*How Britain is Governed—Anglo-Saxon Primer*—who on earth reads all these? I thought you said they only read shockers?"

"That is virtually true," said Bethell sadly. "They make a show of taking their Tripos books with them, but they never open them. Tom, how much constitutional history have you read since you left Cambridge?"

"Oh, a bit, now and then," said Scorby awkwardly.

"About three pages a fortnight, eh? Well, never mind. I'm not examining you now. . . . The Bantu dialects—hideous things!—would be Bonzo's. He intends to be a proconsul in Nigeria, or wherever the Bantus reside. The Anglo-Saxon grammar and this,"—he pulled down a volume of Du Chaillu's *Viking Age*—"are Robert's, I fancy."

"Are they, now?" said MacNair. "Was he intending to take up a job in Iceland or some such place?"

"I don't think so. It's one of these new-fangled Triposes—Archaeology and Anthropology, I believe. Heaven knows why Robert wanted to read for it. Perhaps he thought it was a course of study that would provide him with a degree with the minimum of effort. If that was the case, he was sadly mistaken. It's a brute of a Tripos, or so I am informed."

"Hmm," said MacNair. He absently replaced the *Anglo-Saxon Primer* on the shelf. This was all very well, but not quite what he was after.

"Tell me," he said, turning to Scorby, "where are all these detective stories you read so many of?"

"They came from Brown's library. Cox took them back just now."

"I see. You had a subscription there?"

"Nearly all of us had subscriptions. It only costs threepence a volume, and you pay half a crown, which you get back. I say, Guzzle," he added, as a sudden suspicion crossed his mind, "you got our half-crown deposits back, I hope?"

"Of course I did."

"Well, mind you give them all back to the right people," said Scorby warningly. "In fact, I'll have my half-crown now, if you don't mind."

After a further but cursory examination of the room, MacNair took his leave. Quitting the house, he walked down the hill and along the High Street until he saw, on the opposite side of the street, the gaily decorated shop-front that proclaimed itself a branch of the great bookselling firm of W. J. Brown and Sons.

In the circulating library upstairs, he addressed himself to an elderly, capable-looking lady who sat behind a desk piled high with books.

"Am I correct in supposing that some members of the Cambridge crew had subscriptions here?"

"They may have had," replied the lady shortly.

"Would it be asking too much," pursued MacNair suavely, "to be allowed to see some of the books they took out?"

"It would indeed," said the lady, shutting her mouth with a snap and retiring behind her stockade of books.

MacNair advanced once more to the attack. "It is a matter of some importance, madam. I am——"

"I know very well what you are," interrupted the lady. "I know your sort. You want to steal one of the books you think that poor murdered boy was reading, to gloat over it as a souvenir." She darted an indignant glare at him through her spectacles.

"I was about to say, madam," said MacNair, "that I am a Detective Inspector from Scotland Yard, in charge of this case. Here are my credentials." He drew a card from his pocket and laid it on the desk.

"Oh!" exclaimed the lady, thawing at once. "The police! Why ever didn't you say so? I read all about you in the report of that dreadful inquest. I hope you have the miscreant safely under lock and key! Too dreadful to think that such a nice boy could be killed in cold blood— although if he was in a hot bath at the time, as they say, you could hardly call it cold blood, could you? I always think . . ."

"Exactly, madam. I quite agree with you," said MacNair. "Now, might I see your records of the books taken out by any of the Cambridge men?"

"We are not supposed to tell people anything about our customers," said the lady, "but of course if it's the police it's different, isn't it? I suppose it's what you call a hanging matter, isn't it?"

"It is," replied MacNair gravely.

The lady gave a little shudder, and produced a large book filled with entries in pencil.

"Here you are. Subscriptions were taken out under the names of Ramsey, Gawsell, Tatersale, Salvago, Lloyd, Kirkpatrick and Scorby, but the little cox, Mr. Gawsell, was the one I saw most often. He used to come here to change the books for the others, and he returned all the books only an hour or two ago. You might have seen him if you had come in then. The poor dead boy, he was never in here at all, that I remember, but some of them took out books under the others' subscriptions and said it didn't matter, but it made it so confusing for us, didn't it? The subscriptions all began about a fortnight ago, when the crew came to Putney. You will see the titles of all the books here, under the various names. Nearly all fiction, you see, and mostly detective stories. So dreadful to think of them reading all these tales of murder and sudden death, and then for a thing like this to happen right amongst them! Such a lesson, don't you think?"

MacNair bent over the list of titles. It was much as he had expected. A number of Edgar Wallace's, of course. *The Singing Bone* and *The Case-Book of Dr. Thorndyke,* by R. Austin Freeman. *The Trail of the Lotto,* by Anthony Armstrong. Two or three Agatha Christies. *Lord Peter Views the Body,* by Dorothy Sayers. Two A. E. W. Masons. *The Cask, The Groote Park Murder,* and *The Man From the Sea,* by Freeman Wills Crofts. *The Noose* and *The Rasp,* by Philip MacDonald. *The Three Taps,* by Ronald Knox.

"A pretty good assortment," he murmured. "What a feast of blood and slaughter! No wonder they got talking about murders."

"Yes, isn't it *awful—*" began the lady. MacNair shut the book with a slap, and straightened himself. "I have seen what I want now," he said. "Thank you so much." Evading the lady's eager questions, he rapidly descended the stairs.

In the shop below, he paused to purchase a shilling edition of one of the books which had figured in the list he had just inspected. Pocketing this, he walked back to the crew's old quarters.

He was just in time to catch Gawsell and Scorby, who were packing the last load of suit-cases and parcels into a car that stood outside the door.

"Back again," he said. "I just wanted to ask you something, cox. Have you ever read this book?" As he spoke, he produced his recent purchase.

"No, I don't think I have," said Gawsell, taking the book, and looking at him in bewilderment.

"I am prepared to believe that," said MacNair. "If you had read it, you would have told me all about it, I feel sure. But a copy of this book was taken out of Brown's library a fortnight ago, in your name."

"Oh, that's it, is it?" replied the coxswain. "I took out the books for most of the crew, and we never bothered much whose name they were taken out in. As far as I remember, Lloyd read that one. Probably several of them read it, because I remember seeing it about the place for some days. But it was a different copy—a fat, seven-and-sixpenny one. Is it a clue?"

"Yes; and you, indirectly, put me on to it," answered MacNair. "Don't ask me more; and if you happen to read it in the next few days, keep your ideas to yourself."

"Come on, Tom," said Gawsell. "We'll leave the car for a bit."

"Where are you going?"

"To Brown's."

"Now I wonder whether I should have told them that much?" mused MacNair, as he watched the pair disappear down the hill. With a little sigh, he turned and followed them, in search of a bus.

CHAPTER TEN

Robert Tatersale listlessly raised his head as MacNair entered the cell. His square, bulldog face was drawn and pale under the tan which the buffetings of wind and spray had imposed in long wintry afternoons on Cam and Thames. He eyed the detective dully as he spoke.

"Well?" he asked. "What's up now? Found more so-called evidence? Full confession in my own handwriting discovered artfully concealed under the bath-mat, or what?"

"There's no need to be bitter," replied MacNair quietly. "Believe me, I haven't come here to badger you."

Tatersale grunted sceptically.

"I only want to ask you a few questions about that spanner."

"I've already told you once to-day that I never saw the beastly thing," said Tatersale irritably.

"I want you to think again. The spanner, I find, is one that is missing from the boat-house. It is a common tool there, used for altering riggers. You must have seen it about."

"I knew that was what it was, of course," said Tatersale. "But there are so many tools of that sort knocking about a boat-house, that I naturally wasn't going to say I had had anything to do with that particular one. There are a score of boat-houses along Putney Embankment that it might have come from. How am I to know anything about it?"

"Look here, Tatersale," said MacNair earnestly. "Don't think that I am trying to trap you into any admission. Although I am a police officer, and responsible for this case, I may tell you frankly that I am not as satisfied as some people—as the Coroner's jury, for instance—that your fingerprints came on that spanner in the manner suggested at the inquest. I am at present working on a line of my own. For reasons which ought to be fairly obvious to you, I am not going to tell you what that line is; but I can say this, that if there proves to be anything in it, it will help you rather than hurt you. So come on."

Tatersale looked keenly at the other. "Well. . ." he began.

"Well, what?"

Tatersale shrugged his shoulders hopelessly. "I don't know what I was going to say. The whole business beats me all ends up. The more I think about it, the less sense I can make of it, until I almost feel I'm going potty."

"Suppose I ask a question or two, to start you off," said MacNair. "In the first place, who is in the habit of using these tools at the boat-house ? Is it only the boatmen and their assistants?"

"No. We all use them at various times—the coaches, the cox, and I more than the rest. There's a lot of tinkering with the boat that can't be left to the boatmen alone. Take a spanner, like that wretched one that's causing all the bother, for instance. When we packed up to leave Henley, three or four of us—I can't remember who—helped to unship the riggers from the boat we were using there, and we used that type of spanner for the work. We had more than one of them, I know."

"Then wasn't it rather foolish of you to deny flatly that you had ever seen such a thing?"

"I didn't say that. I said I had never, to my certain knowledge, seen that particular one. How could I be sure of it, when they all look alike?"

"Well, never mind that now," said MacNair. "I want you to cast your mind back over the last few days, and tell me whether you can remember using, or seeing any one else use, a spanner of that type quite recently."

Tatersale puckered his brows. "It's some time since a rigger has been altered," he replied. "We haven't touched any since we shifted the crew round and put in Salvago at seven. That was when we first arrived at Putney."

"Could anybody have altered a rigger since then without your knowledge?"

"Certainly not."

"Well," pursued MacNair, "what is the last time you remember using tools of any sort at the boat-house?"

"Four days ago, on Monday," was the prompt answer. "We got back from a week-end at East-bourne in the morning, and after lunch we had an outing. I went down a bit early, as there were one or two things I wanted to see to."

"Such as?"

"Well, I wanted to rasp my oar-handle for one thing, and then I wanted to have stroke's stretcher moved a bit. He found it was too long, or thought it was."

"Did any one go with you?"

Tatersale hesitated for a perceptible moment. "Yes," he replied. "Er— one of the fellows—never mind who—wanted to do some messing about on his own account, so he came."

"Was there anybody else in the boat-house?"

"No. Dursfield ought to have been there, but he didn't turn up until we had been there some time. Willie arrived later, as he had gone to Cambridge for the week-end to see his wife."

"Was Hardstaff there?"

"That pimply little blighter? No. He's never there when he's wanted. This other bloke and I had to fend for ourselves."

"Now, Tatersale," said MacNair, "tell me as carefully as you can exactly what happened."

"Oh, nothing happened," said Tatersale, looking mystified. "I messed about a bit, pottering about, you know; and so did—the other chap. He wanted to hammer in a nail that was sticking out on the sax-board of his sculling-boat ..."

"Sculling-boat, eh?" interrupted MacNair. "So it was Lloyd, the spare man, then?"

"Well, yes, it was," said the other, in some confusion. "I didn't want to bring his name in because—oh, well, because you're a Robert and all that, and, to be honest, I never quite know what you're up to. It's bad enough for me to be in this silly fix, without dragging some other poor bloke into it."

"Don't be a fool," said MacNair angrily. "This is no time for schoolboy codes of honour. Can't you realise that this may be a matter of life and death?"

"Well, I don't suppose it matters much what his name was anyway," said Tatersale. "All that happened was, as I was saying, that he wanted to hammer in a nail that was sticking out. And he did it. That's all."

"I see. Didn't ask you to hand him any tools or anything, did he ?"

"Ask me to hand him tools? No, I don't think so. . . . Yes, wait a bit. He said he couldn't find a hammer, so he asked me to chuck him some tool or other that was lying beside me on the bench. I was working at the bench, you see, with my back turned to him, so I didn't see much of what he was doing."

"What sort of tool was it you handed him?"

"Oh, Lord, I don't know," replied Tatersale wearily. "Something he could biff in a nail with. I don't see what on earth all this has to do with my being locked up here, or with old Alan's death."

"Don't you?" said MacNair. "Well, it has a bearing on the case. I hope, for your sake, a strong bearing." He rose, and held out his hand. "Well, good-bye, old man."

Tatersale took the outstretched hand, and looked at the other. For the first time, a spark of hope seemed to gleam in his eyes.

"I don't know what you're driving at, Inspector," he said, "but I know I can trust you to get at the real secret of this ghastly mess. Good-bye, and good luck to you."

Twenty minutes later, MacNair was walking along Putney Embankment in the gathering dusk. The tide was out, and the river, a constricted stream, gleamed dully as it serpented between broad, dismal wastes of mud. Most of the boat-houses had now been locked up for the night, and MacNair had small hopes of catching any of the boatmen.

Presently an indistinct figure came in sight, and revealed itself as the lad Hardstaff, slouching towards the lights of Putney High Street with a drooping cigarette dangling from his lower lip. MacNair stopped him.

" 'Evening," he said. "Wait a moment—don't go yet. I want to ask you something. Where were you on Monday, after lunch?"

Fear glinted in the boy's fish-like eyes, and he shuffled as he answered.

"I weren't nowhere, sir. Leastways, I had lunch at 'ome, not being wanted at the boat-'ouse till three, which was when they said they was going out, and they was away in the morning. I got 'ere just after three—well, twenty past, say—and they'd gone out already. Mr. Dursfield didn't 'arf clout me on the ear neither, for being late."

"I see," said MacNair. "Where is Willie now?"

"Mr. Edwards? 'E's gone 'ome, to 'is lodgings. 'E'll be going back to Cambridge with the boats to-morrow."

"Well, where can I find Dursfield?"

"In the bar of the 'Crown and Sceptre,' I expec', sir."

"Right," said MacNair. "That's all. Now cut along home—and behave yourself, mind."

In a corner of the snuggery of the garish great public-house, MacNair found the little boatman, a glass of beer in front of him.

"Good evening, Mr. Dursfield," said the detective pleasantly. "I just want a quiet word or two with you, if I may. What will you drink?"

Dursfield hurriedly emptied his glass, to make room for the fresh one ordered by MacNair, who seated himself on the bench beside him.

"Well, sir, what can I do for you ? Nice evenin', ain't it?"

"Very. Now, Mr. Dursfield, I just want you to refresh my memory a bit about that spanner, if you don't mind."

"That there spanner, sir? After you showed it to me, I read all about it in the evenin' paper, then I saw what you was gettin' at about it. My word, that was a shockin' business! 'Ooder thought it! And Mr. Tatersale, 'e was always so nice-spoken, too!"

"I'm sure he was. Now, did you see anybody with that spanner on Monday last?"

"Monday, sir?" Dursfield looked troubled. "Well, p'raps I did, p'raps I didn't. I can't rightly say, sir."

"At what time did you get back to the boat-house that afternoon?"

Dursfield paused, and took a long drink before replying.

"Well, sir, p'raps I oughter've told you before, but I didn't like to, quite, not seein' what it had to do with this 'ere murder, and not wishful to get nobody into no trouble. It was this way, see, sir. I was in this bar 'ere, 'avin' a quiet drink like, when, just at closin' time, I remembers that Mr. Lampson 'e wanted me at the boat-'ouse early after lunch, because Willie wouldn't be back from Cambridge in time for the outin'. So I nips back to the boat-'ouse, and, when I get to the door, I sees Mr. Tatersale and Mr. Lloyd messin' about at the workbench. So I didn't want to rush in, and 'ave Mr. Tatersale tick me off for not bein' there, see, so I says to myself, I says, I'll do some work in my little shed at the side, and pretend I've been there all the while, see? So that's what I did."

"Quite natural," said MacNair. "Now, what was Mr. Lloyd doing when you looked in?"

"Mr. Lloyd, sir? 'E was messin' with 'is scullin'-boat. I 'eard 'im say to Mr. Tatersale: ' 'Ere, I want to biff this 'ere nail in,' 'e says, 'chuck me a 'ammer.' Mr. Tatersale, 'e says: 'I ain't got one 'ere.' Then Mr. Lloyd, 'e looks round and says: 'Never mind, that there spanner will do.' So Mr. Tatersale, without lookin', tosses the spanner over. I was goin' to stop 'em from usin' my spanners, or Willie's, for 'ammers, but I says to myself, I'd better lay low, so I went away quiet after that."

"That's most interesting, Mr. Dursfield," said MacNair. "Another pint? Right you are." He gave the order, and continued:

"I want you to think carefully. Did Tatersale throw the spanner holding it by the handle, and did Lloyd catch it by the handle?"

Dursfield scratched his head meditatively. "I don't rightly remember about Mr. Tatersale, sir," he replied. "But Mr. Lloyd, I remember 'im catchin' the spanner by the neck. I remember that, because 'e did it so cleverlike. I didn't see what 'e did after that, 'cause I slipped off to my shed then."

MacNair rubbed his hands together. "Splendid," he said. "Just what I wanted. But don't you go talking about this to anybody, mind."

He remained for a few minutes longer, chatting on general subjects, then departed, leaving a sorely puzzled boatman behind him. In a satisfied frame of mind he walked across the bridge to the Underground station. "A good day's work," he murmured. "A nice evening with a novel will just round it off." He smacked the book in his pocket as he spoke.

CHAPTER ELEVEN

"Hang it all, MacNair," said the Superintendent irritably. "I was going to congratulate you on a quick arrest in this Boat Race affair, and to own myself in the wrong for saying that it couldn't be anything but accident or suicide. Now you have the face to come and tell me that you think you have arrested the wrong man. Really, it's too bad."

"I'm sorry, sir, but——"

"Bah! A nice thing to come and tell me, first thing in the morning. If he was the wrong man, what did you arrest him for, hey?"

"I had no alternative, after the jury's verdict."

"Then you shouldn't have let the jury bring in such a verdict. You can't have coached the Coroner properly. You had no business to let the Coroner drag all that evidence about the fingerprints out of you. The rawest country flattie would have known better, I hope. Simmonds had no business to be at the inquest at all. You should have kept all your material under your hat, if you weren't sure of your case."

MacNair sighed patiently, but was silent.

"Really, I can't make out what you are getting at," continued his superior, taking up a sheaf of papers. "I have carefully read the report of the inquest, and your report of the case against Tatersale, and it looks pretty straightforward to me. A weapon found with blood on it, and the fellow's finger-prints on it—what could be clearer? You haven't much of a motive, but you'll find one if you look for it hard enough. So what on earth is your trouble now?"

MacNair pulled from his pocket the little blue-covered book which he had bought the day before, and laid it on the desk. "My trouble is concerned with that," he said.

The Superintendent picked it up and glanced at the title. " ' *The Rasp,* by Philip MacDonald,' " he read. "Detective yarn, eh? Where did it come from?"

"I bought it yesterday, at Brown's in Putney High Street."

"Well?"

"I read it some years ago, sir, when it first came out, and I read it again last night, to refresh my memory."

"Good Lord!" exploded the Superintendent. "Is your brain going soft, or what? I can't waste my time discussing the literary merits of detective

94

stories with you. I never read the beastly things, except to laugh at them. Take your ridiculous book away! I don't want it."

"I'm sorry, sir," said MacNair. "I began at the wrong end. I found out yesterday that nearly all the Cambridge crew were in the habit of reading a good many detective stories. This book, amongst others, had been recently borrowed by them from Brown's library, and several of them, including Owen Lloyd, the spare man, read it. At any rate, Lloyd certainly did; I can't be sure of the others. I am more inclined to believe that he saw to it that none of the others read it."

"Well, what about it?"

"In this story," MacNair explained patiently, "a murder is committed in an ingenious way. Put shortly, it is this. A man is found with his skull fractured by a vicious blow. Near the body is found a wood-rasp, a sort of heavy file. On the handle are the finger-prints of a certain man, whom we can call X. It later turned out that the murder had really been committed by another man, Z. This man had a carpenter's shop, in which he was constantly working. One day, when X happened to be there, Z asked him to hand him a certain tool, which he did. Afterwards, Z carefully removed the handle of this tool, which bore X's fingerprints, and preserved it. When the right moment came, he hit his victim over the head with the rasp, holding it by its shank without a handle. When he had done this, he fitted his handle to the rasp, without disturbing the fingerprints, and left it on the spot. And there you are—blood-stained weapon, complete with finger-prints of X. Obviously X is guilty."

"I begin to see what you are driving at," said the Superintendent. "Go on."

"By a bit of luck, I was able to get yesterday the evidence of a boatman, who witnessed a very pretty little scene down at the Cambridge boathouse on Monday." He described what Dursfield had told him. "So you see, sir, Lloyd followed almost exactly the procedure of Z in the story, but without one of the refinements. Z got X to handle the wooden handle when it was attached, not to the rasp with which he, Z, afterwards committed the crime, but to some tool of quite a different sort; so that the unfortunate X never saw the rasp at all, until it was found with his apparently damning finger-prints on the handle, which had been transferred to it. Now, Lloyd did not do this. Perhaps he found it impossible to fit his handle to another sort of tool, or perhaps his plot was unpremeditated, and it was only when he found himself alone in the boathouse with Tatersale that the possibility of staging a crime on the lines of the one he had read about suggested itself. Who knows? It may be that the idea flashed through his brain at the very moment that the spanner, tossed to him by the President, was sailing through the air. He caught it dexterously by the shank—I have Dursfield's evidence for this—and laid it down carefully. Probably he hammered in his nail with some other tool he had at hand; for, remember, Tatersale's back was turned, and he did not see what Lloyd was doing. Unfortunately for us, Dursfield went away at that moment, or he might have been able to give us some further valuable evidence. Anyway, this is what I fancy must have happened. Presently the rest of the crew came down for their outing, and Tatersale went away to change, leaving Lloyd still tinkering with his sculling-boat. Lloyd, you see, as spare man was master of his own time. He did not go out in the eight with the others, but took his exercise by himself in his sculling-boat. Thus he would have ample opportunity to put his precious spanner, with its finger-prints, to one side, and to pack it for transportation up to the house, in such a way that the prints would not be damaged.

"I said just now that Lloyd's scheme lacked one of the refinements of Z's," MacNair continued. "But in one way he had an advantage over the chap in the book. For Z was the only person in the story who ever used the carpenter's shop; therefore, once it was realised that there might have been some hanky-panky with those finger-prints, everything pointed straight to Z. The rasp was one of his tools, and he was the only man who ever used them. But in this case it is very different. The tools at the boat-house were constantly used by the whole crew, the coaches, and the boatmen, so that nothing at all would point to Lloyd were it not for two things: the fact that Tatersale was able to tell me, without any prompting, or scarcely any, the story of Lloyd's asking him to throw him the tool, and the corroboration of this story, quite independently, by Dursfield. Dursfield's presence unseen was a sheer piece of luck, good for us and bad for Lloyd.

"Then Lloyd, once he had got his spanner, proceeded in much the same way that I first imagine Tatersale did. He roused Strayler out of bed, and invented some pretext for a quiet talk, suggesting that Strayler should pretend to take a bath in order to account for his being up after bedtime. His method here departed totally from the murder in the story. Z's weapon was a heavy wood-rasp, not a comparatively light thing like the spanner. He engaged his unsuspecting victim in conversation, and dealt him a savage blow from behind, killing him instantly. He then arranged the furniture to suggest that a struggle had taken place, upsetting a clock which he manipulated in such a way as to make it appear that X had done it in order to fake an alibi for himself. In our case, of course, nobody has an alibi. Almost any one in the house might have done it.

"Lloyd, I fancy, was too astute to follow the murder in *The Rasp* in every detail, fearing that somebody might notice the resemblance. So he invented instead all this rigmarole of bath-tubs and straps, and knocking Strayler silly for a moment with a light blow, instead of smashing his skull in with a heavy blow. Then he hid the spanner in the bushes—a neat touch, much better than merely leaving the tell-tale weapon by the side of the body. He knew perfectly well that it would be found sooner or later. There was the risk of course, that the fingerprints might be obliterated by the weather or by careless handling; but, even if they were obliterated, there was still nothing to point to him as the guilty person.

"I am beginning to think rather highly of our Mr. Lloyd. He seems to have the Celtic imagination developed to the full. He borrows his idea of wangled finger-prints from a novel, but he drags in a lot of original details of his own, to put us off the scent. In fact, I should never have got on the track had it not been for one or two remarks dropped by Gawsell yesterday."

"That poisonous little cox?" said the Superintendent. "What did he say?"

"In the first place, he told me about some detective story he had read about bogus finger-prints that were forged by means of something on the lines of a rubber stamp. Of course, that idea was preposterous in a case like this, but it set me thinking. Then he told me that not only he, but most of the others, read a good many detective stories. The two ideas, put together, suddenly reminded me of this book, *The Rasp,* which I vaguely remembered having read some time ago. So I at once took steps to find out whether *The Rasp* had been taken from Brown's library by any of the crew, and I found that it had. Gawsell himself had taken it out, but he told me he didn't read it himself. He got it for Lloyd."

"Hmm," commented the Superintendent. "Said he hadn't read it himself, eh? A bit thin, don't you think? Would such an avid devourer of these pestilential shockers have gone to the trouble of borrowing a promising-looking one from a library, and not read it himself?"

"I don't think he can have read it," replied MacNair. "If he had, he would certainly have cited it to me as a case in point, instead of the other more far-fetched yarn about celluloid stamps and camel's blood."

"Camel's blood! Good Lord!" said the Superintendent with a snort.

"Besides, there was nothing unusual in his taking out a book for one of the others to read. Apparently he did most of the shopping for the crew. Probably Lloyd asked him to get him a detective story of some sort, and he got this one, which gave Lloyd his idea."

"So you have only Gawsell's word for it that Lloyd and not he read the book?"

"Yes, sir. I see what you mean. But Gawsell is a little sprat, who couldn't possibly have engineered a crime of this sort. Also, there is Dursfield's evidence of the scene in the boat-house."

"Have you looked at the spanner again?" the Superintendent asked. "Does it show any signs of monkeying such as you suggest?"

In answer, MacNair produced a cardboard box, from which he drew the instrument in question.

"You see, sir," he said, fingering it, "the handle comes off fairly easily, but not so easily that the shank would fly off if it were roughly handled. The shank is quite small in diameter, so I don't think that Lloyd used it without a handle, as the man in the book used his rasp. He would need a handle of some sort to get a proper grip; and I fancy he borrowed a handle for the purpose from the boat-house. I saw several loose wooden handles lying about amongst the tools and odds and ends there, and probably he took one of those. If we could find such a handle anywhere about at the house, it would strengthen our case, of course. This morning I telephoned to Jevons, and asked him to have another thorough search made of the house and grounds. But Lloyd will have had the sense to hide it very carefully, or even to destroy it if possible. It's too much, I suppose, to hope to find the thing with his own finger-prints on it."

The Superintendent sat back in his chair. "This is all most ingenious, MacNair," he said. "Of course you have evidence of motive on Lloyd's part?"

MacNair was somewhat embarrassed in his reply. "Well, sir, of course it was only late yesterday afternoon that I began working on this new line, and I haven't much to go on as yet. But there is the beginning of a motive, I think, in Lloyd's soreness at having been turned out of the crew, as I told you on Thursday."

"Was he turned out in favour of Strayler?"

"No. Salvago got his place."

"And you have nothing else?"

"Not at present."

"Good heavens, man!" exclaimed the Superintendent. "Do you mean to say you have wasted all this time on such utterly trivial grounds? You say you have no motive, save that the fellow was disgruntled at being turned out of the crew. In that case, if he was the sort of man to want revenge, he would want revenge on the people who turned him out—the President, and the coach. But why should he want to harm Strayler? It isn't even as though Strayler was the man who supplanted him in the boat. You have nothing at all to show why he should want to murder Strayler—your whole case is built up on some fanciful resemblance between Lloyd's actions at the boat-house and the behaviour of some silly puppet in a novel."

He glared at his subordinate, and went on: "You are as bad as Gawsell, you know. He comes rushing to you with some ridiculous theory drawn from a story-book, and that sets you off on a theory of your own drawn from some other book! Good Lord, man, you have only Gawsell's word for it that Lloyd read the book. He may never have set eyes on it—this little shrimp Gawsell may be having a game with you all the time! Ugh! You make me sick!"

MacNair was about to speak, but the Superintendent silenced him with a gesture. "Wait a moment. I haven't finished. Your case is based on the fact, reported by a boatman who had been spending an hour or so in a pub by his own admission, that Lloyd asked Tatersale to throw him a spanner. What of it? If every person who asks some one else to hand him a tool is to be suspected of murder, you would have to arrest the whole Cambridge crew, and half the population of London as well. I suppose I have asked you to hand me things on dozens of occasions. That doesn't make me a murderer, does it?"

"No, sir. But the fact that this scene was enacted at the boat-house, two days before the murder, together with the fact that the same spanner, as far as we can judge, was found with blood on it, also Tatersale's finger-prints, and the fact that Lloyd read this novel only a week or so ago. . . ."

"According to Gawsell."

". . . According to Gawsell, whose word I have no reason to doubt; these facts, taken in conjunction, seem to me to present a strong *prima facie* case against Lloyd. I am not, at this stage, asserting dogmatically that Lloyd did commit the crime in this way; I am merely pointing out that he could have done it, and that the case against Tatersale is thereby seriously weakened."

"If we have to admit that you made a bloomer in arresting Tatersale," said the Superintendent, "there will be a fearful outcry, as you know. The papers are making enough fuss as it is. . . . The responsibility is yours; what do you propose to do now?"

"I propose, sir, to find out what I can about Lloyd. Cambridge, I fancy, must be my hunting-ground. I can just catch the eleven-fifty if I go now."

"Go ahead," said the Superintendent; then, as MacNair was about to open the door, he called to him. "Here, take your shilling shocker out of my room." He tossed the small book lightly to the other.

"MacNair!" he called again, when the door had shut.

"Sir?" said the Inspector, returning.

"You have my finger-prints on it now," chuckled the Superintendent sardonically. "Don't go leaving it about near any corpses."

Some two hours later, MacNair alighted on the long Cambridge platform and inquired the whereabouts of the college of which Owen Lloyd was a member. The ticket-collector told him that it was some distance away, and advised him to take a bus; MacNair, however, decided to walk, for he had lunched on the train, and he had some time to kill before he could expect to find any of the college officials free to receive him. Accordingly he sauntered slowly along the interminable thoroughfare of shops that leads to the centre of the town; lost himself; was obliged to ask his way several times; and finally, at two o'clock, arrived in sight of the mellow stone gateway of the college, and applied for information to a staid, top-hatted porter.

"If you wished any information concerning members of the college you should apply to the senior tutor," said the porter. "Here is Mr. Blessington, the senior tutor, now. You had better speak to him, sir."

MacNair turned and saw a tall figure striding across the grass, his black gown fluttering behind him. Unconscious of his solecism, he hurried across the lawn to intercept him.

"Might I have a few words with you privately, sir, on an important matter?"

The tutor, a spare, sandy-haired man, slackened his steps. "Certainly," he replied. Then, indicating with a smile the porter who hovered, a picture of outraged dignity, in the background, he added: "I fear you have unwittingly committed a heinous offence in the eyes of our good porter. The fact is, the grass is supposed to be sacred to fellows of the college—and their guests," he went on, as MacNair started to apologise. "If you will come up to my rooms, I can give you a few minutes."

He led the way across the spacious court and up a short flight of stairs to a pleasant room, low and panelled with age-darkened oak. Through the mullioned windows MacNair could see tall elms, and a glimpse of a narrow, sluggish river beyond.

"And what can I do for you, Mr.—?" queried the tutor, when they had seated themselves.

"MacNair, Detective-Inspector MacNair of Scotland Yard." The detective handed his card to the other, who lifted an eyebrow in surprise. "I am in charge of the investigations arising out of the death of Alan Strayler, the Cambridge stroke."

"Really!" exclaimed Blessington. "A shocking affair! We in Cambridge, of course, know only what has been published in the newspapers, but, from what we can learn, it seems a truly ghastly tragedy. It will give such unfortunate notoriety to the University."

"It will, I am afraid," agreed MacNair.

"And such an opportunity to these Socialist spouters! . . . But you will forgive me, Inspector, if I express my wonderment at your coming to me. Surely the poor lad who died, and the other boy who has been arrested, belong to another college ?"

"That is true. But several others of the crew are members of this college, are they not?"

"Yes, indeed. Scorby, Ramsey, and Lloyd, the ninth man, are all from this college. They are not implicated, I hope?" asked the tutor, in alarm.

MacNair chose his words diplomatically. "They are only implicated in the sense that they were members of the crew, and present on the fatal night. You must understand, sir, that it is the duty of the police to investigate fully every avenue."

"And leave no stone unturned—is not that the phrase?" said the tutor. "Unfortunately," he added with a sigh, "the upturning of stones generally reveals nothing but crawling nastiness. . . . Still, I must help you if I can. I am sure that our two Blues have nothing to fear from the most searching inquiry. They are both fine young fellows; not, perhaps, as ripe in scholarship as one might wish, but unexceptionable in their behaviour."

"Is it by intention that you confine your remarks to the two actual Blues?" MacNair asked.

The tutor hesitated perceptibly. "I should be loth to say anything that might give you false ideas about Lloyd," he said. "At the same time, I am afraid that I cannot in fairness give him the same character that I am happy to give the other two. I do not think I need say any more."

"You must realise, Mr. Blessington," said MacNair, assuming his best Scotland Yard manner, "that this is an extremely serious matter. A young man, an undergraduate of your University, is in custody on a capital charge. Either that charge must be substantiated, or he must be cleared of all suspicion and released. I may tell you in confidence that the police are not entirely satisfied about your pupil, Lloyd, and would like to know a little more about him. So I must ask you to be good enough to expand what you hinted at just now."

"Well, Inspector," replied the tutor, "there is not very much to say. Certainly Lloyd has never, to my knowledge, committed a breach of any laws other than our own disciplinary regulations. But I must tell you that the college authorities are far from satisfied with his conduct. He has attached himself to a rather foolish set of young men, with far more money at their disposal than he has, who live expensively and spend far too much of their time at race meetings. Lloyd's parents are both dead, I believe, so that there is no parental bar to his spending such money as he possesses as he pleases, and this he has been in the habit of doing, rather recklessly. As you may be aware, we have a regulation which compels Cambridge tradesmen to furnish to the college the names of undergraduates whose unpaid accounts amount to more than five pounds, at the end of each term. Lloyd has been a constant offender in this respect, and we have often had to remonstrate with him. He undoubtedly owes considerable amounts in London and elsewhere, but of course such debts do not come officially to our notice. Shortly before he left Cambridge with the crew I had occasion to speak to him very seriously. I warned him that he was leading an idle life, and living beyond his means, and told him that the college might be forced to take drastic steps if he persisted in his conduct."

"What did he say?"

"I am sorry to say that he treated my remonstrances lightly, and made some foolish remark about hoping to make what he described as a 'packet' on the Grand National, which I understand is a horse race. He offered to tell me the name of the animal which he favoured, but I told him that such levity was ill-timed."

"You don't know the horse's name, then?" MacNair asked.

"I believe I remember it. I think it was Hot Baby, which struck me as a preposterous name for a horse."

"And Hot Baby crashed at Becher's Brook—a week ago, before the murder," mused the detective.

"He also told me," Blessington continued, "that he had every prospect of shortly receiving a very large sum of money under a will, which would enable him to pay his debts. But only a year ago he inherited a considerable sum, under the same will, I believe. The money was left to him outright, and I fear that, in vulgar parlance, he ran through it very quickly."

"This is interesting," said MacNair. "Do you happen to know any further details about this will?"

"No, except that I believe the money was left him by an uncle. He did not tell me why he should have received one sum of money last year, and another this year, although it struck me as peculiar."

"Can you tell me anything else about him?"

"There is nothing of importance that I can think of. Lloyd has never been guilty of anything more serious than foolish and thoughtless behaviour. There have never, I am happy to say, been any complaints of rowdiness, drunkenness, or anything of that nature."

"I am glad to hear that," said MacNair. "In any case, I should imagine that young men who went in for that sort of thing would hardly be in the running for places in the University boat. . . . Now, there is one thing more, Mr. Blessington. I suppose Lloyd has a set of rooms in the college. Would it be possible for me to have a quiet look at them?"

The tutor pursed his lips. "What you ask is most unusual, Inspector," he demurred. "You have not a search warrant, I suppose?"

"Oh, dear no," answered MacNair cheerfully. "My suspicions aren't definite enough to apply for one of those. I only want a little peep round. You might put it that I want to look at a set of rooms for . . . for my nephew, who may be coming up next October."

"But would that not be a falsehood?" asked Blessington gravely.

"Not exactly. I have a nephew, really. He has just started work in the City; but, for all I can tell, my brother-in-law might suddenly decide to send the boy up to Cambridge. You never know, do you ?"

"I don't quite like this, Inspector," said the tutor. "But, as it is an important matter, I might perhaps connive at your little *supercherie.*"

He turned to his desk and scribbled a short note, which he handed to the detective. "If you give this to the head porter, he will let you have the key of Lloyd's rooms, C2, New Court."

MacNair thanked him, and rose to depart.

"One moment, Inspector," called Blessington, as he was about to go. "I remember now what Lloyd said to me."

"Yes?" said MacNair, with interest.

"He advised me to put my shirt on Hot Baby. Those were his words. For a moment I was unable to understand him, for I was at a loss to perceive why a hot baby should require a shirt. Good-bye, Inspector."

A few minutes later, MacNair fitted his key to the heavy, unpanelled "oak" that guarded Owen Lloyd's rooms. Within was a second and lighter door, which was unlocked. On opening this, he found himself in a tiny sitting-room, scantily furnished, like most college rooms, with the plain and battered furniture that had served some twenty previous owners. The ornaments of the room were few. Over the mantelpiece hung an emblazoned oar, which had been won in the May Races of the previous year; on the walls were several rowing groups and one or two sporting prints from paintings by Munnings and Lionel Edwards. A bookshelf held a few tattered volumes, evidently text-books for the History Tripos.

There was a small desk, which was of more interest to MacNair. He tried its only drawer, and to his joy found it unlocked. He drew up a chair, and sat down to examine the contents at leisure.

"Bills—bills—bills," he murmured, turning over the papers. "Our Owen has been going the pace. . . . Bookmaker's circular. Hector Mac-Alexander, of Glasgow. I know him. One of the Jordan Highlanders. . . . Cottenham Steeplechases. . . . Drag. . . . Athenaeum Club. . . . More bills. . . . Hullo! This looks interesting."

His find was a fragment of a letter, of which only the heading and the first few lines remained. Evidently the scrap had been preserved as a reminder of the address of the firm of solicitors who had written the letter. They were Messrs. Frank, Treyer, Kellett and Frank, of 41, Cater Street, Holborn, and the letter was dated the previous February.

"Dear Sir," it began.

"In reply to your letter of the 16th inst., we wish to state once more that under the provisions of the will of our late client, Mr. Thomas Elwyn Lloyd . . ." Here the fragment ended.

MacNair carefully folded the scrap of paper and placed it in his pocket-book. He closed the drawer, leaving its other contents as he had found them. After a glance into the small bedroom, which offered no unusual features, he locked the outer door once more and returned the key to the porter's lodge.

"When I can get a look at that will," he said to himself as he took his seat in the bus which conveyed him to the station, "I shall begin to understand what all this is about."

CHAPTER TWELVE

The following day MacNair was perforce idle; for his next task, he had decided, would be to see the solicitors and discover more about Owen Lloyd's financial position, and for this he would have to wait until Monday. He spent part of the morning amusing himself with the Sunday papers. That eminent publicist, Mr. John Dumbbell, was somewhat hampered by the fact that the case was *sub judice;* nevertheless, with his brush well dipped in his favourite thick and treacly purple pigment, he contrived to daub some characteristic patches. Quivering with the righteousness of a blunt Briton, he danced before the portals of the older Universities, calling loudly upon the inmates to shake off their slimy hypocrisies, to forsake their venerable shams and shibboleths, to abandon their mandarins and mumbo-jumbo, and to take as their models for the future the more democratic educational establishments of the younger countries of the Empire.

On other pages, sandwiched between the autobiographies of an American night club queen and a gentleman who claimed to have been the original cat burglar, the same newspaper published profuse and for the most part inaccurate life-stories of the members of the Cambridge crew, with articles on "Training for the Boat Race," by a former Oxford spare man, and "What the Undergrad Thinks of the Blues," by an alleged Cambridge man. The whole was of course tastefully embellished with photographs of everybody and everything that had the remotest connexion with the "Blue in the Bath Case."

Most of the other newspapers were much the same, and MacNair threw them aside with a yawn. He began to review the case, and to range his thoughts in order. He was now convinced that Lloyd was the true criminal; but from his conviction to a conviction in a court of law—he smiled wryly at the poor pun—was a far step. In his experience he had met far too many cases in which, thanks to an eloquent advocate or to the lack of admissible evidence, undoubted criminals had gone free while the police looked on, powerless. Was this case to be one of these? His evidence was purely circumstantial; would it convince a jury? With stronger evidence of motive, he felt that it might; and something told him that Thomas Lloyd's will held the clue to the secret. Again, it was a pity that the second handle, for which he had hoped, had not been found.

Jevons had telephoned to him the previous evening, after he had returned from Cambridge, to announce his failure.

"We went through that garden with a toothcomb," said Jevons plaintively. "All through the house we looked, too, and not a sight of a handle or anything like it, except for the things in the kitchen, tin-openers and so forth, but I knew that that wasn't what you were after Not even a smell of anything you might call a clue."

"Never mind," sighed MacNair. "It was only an idea of mine. Very likely he didn't use a handle at all."

"By the way," Jevons continued, "when I got there I found Major Lampson and Mr. Bethell strolling about in the garden. The patrol man let them in, as he knew they had always had the run of the place. That was all right, I hope?"

"Oh, quite. Did you tell them what you were looking for?"

"Oh, no, sir." Jevons's voice sounded shocked. "Not a word. I didn't let on that we were looking for anything at all. Just said that I had come to see that the place was all right. They went away soon after I came."

The failure to find the hypothetical handle did not, however, shake MacNair's conviction of the truth of his theory. Perhaps after all Lloyd had held the spanner by the shank. But what, he reflected, was Lloyd's little game exactly? Evidently there was money in it somewhere; quite possibly the money he had hoped to obtain under his uncle's will had failed to materialise, and he had turned to the grisly expedient of murder in order to raise money in some mysterious way which for the moment MacNair could not understand.

A sudden thought struck him. It would be as well to find out something about this uncle, if possible. He turned to an old *Who's Who,* issued three years previously, and soon found the entry he sought.

Thomas Elwyn Lloyd had been born in Cardiff in 1869, evidently the son of well-to-do parents, for he had been educated at Cambridge—at the college of which his nephew was now a member. Moreover, he had rowed for his University, in one of the great Muttlebury's famous crews.

"Now, *that's* interesting," murmured MacNair to himself.

He had then returned to his native land, and had evidently done well in the iron and steel industry, particularly during the war, when he had devoted his energies to the manufacture of munitions. He sat in Parliament as a Coalition Liberal from 1917 to 1922, and received the O.B.E. He had married in 1897, but his wife had died during the war. He possessed what was tersely described as *one d.*

The record went no further, since of course Thomas Lloyd was still living when it was published. MacNair closed the volume.

"So the old boy rowed for Cambridge," he mused once more. "Now, I wonder if that means anything."

Early on the following morning he visited the offices of Frank, Treyer, Kellett and Frank. It is needless to say that there was no Treyer, no Kellett, and not even a solitary Frank on the premises. The senior partner, Mr. Bagworthy, a thin-lipped, desiccated man, received him without warmth.

"This is most unusual, you know, Inspector," he said, when MacNair had briefly stated his business. "I fail to see the slightest connexion between my late client's will and the case which you profess to be investigating. If you obtain an order from a judge in chambers I shall of course be obliged to supply you with the information you wish; but, until then, the interests of my client scarcely permit me to babble of his affairs to every police officer who comes along."

MacNair shrugged his shoulders philosophically. It seemed to him as though he had spent the greater part of the past few days in being told by different people that his actions were most unusual. But what else could one expect, in a case that was itself manifestly most unusual?

He was not, however, at the end of his resources. A few minutes after leaving the lawyer's office he was at Somerset House, and after a brief delay Thomas Lloyd's will was spread before him.

What he saw there made him give a low whistle of surprise. When he had mastered its contents he handed the document back to the attendant and hurried out of the building. He was back at the office in Cater Street as quickly as a bus could carry him.

The solicitor looked at his visitor in some surprise. "You are soon back, Inspector," he said. "I hope you have not wasted your time by returning on the same errand. As I have already told you——"

"I have not wasted my time, Mr. Bagworthy," interrupted MacNair. "I have seen the will, as you must have known that I would; and now I should like you to tell me briefly what you can about the testator's curious bequest to his nephew, Owen Lloyd. I must remind you that I am investigating an extremely serious case. As a solicitor, you are as much an officer of the law as I am; and you will be gravely hampering the course of the law if you withhold this information."

The lawyer sighed. "Very well, Inspector, if you insist," he replied. "The case is really very simple. My late client, Mr. Thomas Lloyd, retired from business some three years ago, and he died a fairly rich man. His original intention was to leave his entire fortune to his daughter, Mrs. Pritchard, except for a few minor bequests and the sum of £ 1,000 to his nephew, Mr. Owen Lloyd, the son of his brother Owen who is now deceased. He had always taken a great interest in the boy, and it was partly through his assistance that he was able to go to Cambridge.

"Only a short time before his death, he heard that Owen had taken up rowing at the University. He was greatly delighted at this, as he had been a prominent oarsman himself. He summoned me, and insisted on altering his will. Owen was now to get £1,000 outright, and another £1,000 if he obtained his Blue, to be paid on the day on which he took part in the Boat Race."

"A curious bequest," commented MacNair.

"An unusual one, certainly," said the lawyer. "It was, however, the whim of an old man, and I had to respect it. I may tell you that Mr. Lloyd, though not very old in years, suffered in health during the last portion of his life, and his mind was no longer as keen as it had been. Of course there was no suggestion, you will understand, that he was not in a fit state to arrange his affairs. He had set his heart on seeing his nephew— since he had no son of his own—row in the Boat Race, as he had done. He told me that if he lived to see this happen, he would himself immediately present his nephew with the £1,000 which he had set apart as the reward, and, of course, alter his will accordingly. But he had a premonition, since justified, that he would die before his nephew could win a seat in the Cambridge eight; and hence the clause in his will."

"Owen Lloyd knew of this clause, of course?" asked MacNair.

"Oh, yes. The will was proved a year ago, and he received his £1,000 then—I mean the first £1,000, which was left to him unconditionally. Very likely also his uncle told him of his intentions before he died."

"If Owen Lloyd does not row in the race, the money goes to charity, does it not?"

"That is so. If he takes his degree and goes down without having taken part in the Boat Race, the £1,000 goes to the hospitals of Cardiff, in addition to £500 which they have already received."

"And this is Owen's last year at Cambridge, and therefore his last chance to win the £1,000, isn't it?"

"I believe that to be the case. He has been there three years, and takes his degree in June."

"Now, Mr. Bagworthy," said MacNair, leaning forward across the desk which separated him from the lawyer, "I want to ask a rather important question. Have you had any correspondence lately with Owen Lloyd about this clause in his uncle's will?"

The other put his finger-tips together and looked at him over the top of his pince-nez. "I am not sure whether I ought to answer that," he replied. "I can see in what direction your questions are tending, and in the interests of my client——"

"In the interests of justice," said MacNair sharply, "you must tell me what you know."

"Well, then," replied Bagworthy reluctantly, "it is true that we have had a certain amount of correspondence, during the past month or two, with Mr. Owen Lloyd."

"Tell me about it."

"As you must have seen from your inspection of the will," the solicitor replied, "the wording is slightly ambiguous. The fault is my own, perhaps. Not being a University man myself, I did not appreciate the finer shades of rowing phraseology, and I followed the wording dictated to me by Mr. Thomas Lloyd. The £1,000 was to go to Owen Lloyd *if he was awarded his Blue,* and the money was to be paid on the day on which he took part in the Oxford and Cambridge Boat Race. We had a letter from him in February, I think, in which he stated that he was then rowing in the University eight, and hoped shortly to receive his Blue. He wished to inquire whether he would still be entitled to the money if, after he had been awarded his colours, he were forced to retire from the crew through illness or any other cause."

"What did you reply?"

"We replied that we did not think he would have any claim to the money in that event. About the middle of March he wrote to us again, from Henley. He said that he had been awarded his Blue, and therefore considered that he was entitled to receive the money even in the event of his not taking part in the race. He evidently had some fear that he might lose his place in the crew—as indeed he did, about a fortnight later. He said in his letter that, if he did not row in the boat, he would almost certainly be spare man, and he considered that this might be construed as taking part in the race. At all events, he asserted, he had been awarded his Blue, which was what the will stipulated."

"And what on earth did you say to that?" asked MacNair, greatly interested.

"A clerk of mine, who was himself a rowing man, suggested a way out of the difficulty. He told me that by tradition no man was counted a Blue until he had actually rowed in the race. The Oxford and Cambridge Presidents 'award Blues' to the new members of the crew, usually when the crew leaves the home waters, as a sign that, *barring the unforeseen*, the crew may then be considered finally settled. But it is only by courtesy that the new men are called Blues, and permitted to wear blue caps and blazers. If any one of them falls ill, or is turned out of the crew before the race, he loses all right to the title and insignia of a Blue. My clerk told me of a number of cases in which this has happened in recent years.

"We therefore wrote to Owen Lloyd and told him that it was clear that if he did not row in the Boat Race he would have no claim to be a Blue, and no claim to the money."

"Did you hear from him again after that?"

"Yes, once," replied the lawyer. "He answered our letter in somewhat intemperate terms—'sharks' was the expression he used—and said that he hoped to regain his seat in the boat, and so get the money in spite of us."

"Did he?" said MacNair significantly. "This is most enlightening."

A look of anxiety crossed the solicitor's face.

"I hope I have acted rightly in telling you this," he said. "You will, I trust, use this information with discretion."

"Certainly," smiled MacNair. "And I hope that you, in return, will keep this little chat to yourself, for the time being at any rate."

An hour later MacNair was closeted with the Superintendent at Scotland Yard.

"Here is a first class motive at last," he said with enthusiasm. "It's all plain as a pikestaff. Lloyd has been going the pace at Cambridge. . . . I don't suppose his fond uncle knew much about that side of his dear nephew's character. He ran through the first £1,000, and he has been desperately hard up. His fancy for the Grand National went west, and all his quibbles wouldn't screw this other thousand out of old Bagworthy unless he actually rows in the race. So he makes up his mind to get back his place in the crew. Nobody will conveniently fall ill; so the dear lad determines to create a vacancy in the crew, by putting Strayler out of the way."

"Why not Salvago—the man who got his place?" asked the Superintendent.

"I don't know. He probably had some good reason. Probably it was easier to out Strayler, and to divert suspicion from himself to Tatersale."

"But——"

"I know what you're going to say. You will tell me that Lloyd is a bow-side oarsman, and that he couldn't stroke the boat. You've been talking to some bright fellow in the Thames Police."

"I have been doing nothing of the sort," said the outraged Superintendent. "I was going to ask you . . ."

"Never mind," interrupted MacNair. "Do please let me get this off my chest before I burst. Scorby is the alternative stroke—I found that out. He would stroke the boat in the event of anything happening to Strayler; Lloyd would go back to his old place at seven, and Salvago would move from seven to six. He can row equally well on either side."

He handed the Superintendent a paper. "I have made out three orders of rowing," he explained. " 'A' is the order in which they rowed during their practice at Henley. 'B' is the amended order, which obtained at the time of the murder. 'C' is the probable order of rowing without Strayler."

The three lists were as follows:

	A.	B.	C.
Bow	Ramsey	Ramsey	Ramsey
2	Westlake	Westlake	Westlake
3	Lightfoot	Lightfoot	Lightfoot
4	Kirkpatrick	Kirkpatrick	Kirkpatrick
5	Tatersale	Tatersale	Tatersale
6	Scorby	Scorby	Salvago
7	Lloyd	Salvago	Lloyd
Str.	Strayler	Strayler	Scorby
Cox.	Gawsell	Gawsell	Gawsell
Spare Man	Salvago	Lloyd	A.N. Other

The Superintendent scanned the lists attentively. "How did you concoct all this?" he asked.

"The first list I got from the newspaper files. The second we all knew already. The third I evolved myself, based on what I learned from Lampson and other sources."

"But look here," objected the Superintendent. "According to your theory, Lloyd's plot included planting clues which would throw suspicion on

Tatersale. If Tatersale is to be suspected of murder, how is he to row five ? In fact, how is the crew to go on at all?"

"In that case," replied MacNair, "I fancy that that hardened veteran, Mr. A. N. Other, would be sent for from Cambridge, and put in the boat somewhere. Lampson told me that, although they had only one spare man on the premises, they had reserves up at Cambridge who could be summoned in case of necessity."

"But that's nonsense. Is it likely that, with the Cambridge President held on a murder charge, practice for the Boat Race would go on as though nothing had happened ? If that theory is correct, why aren't they rowing now?"

"That isn't quite the idea," said MacNair. "I fancy that the casting of suspicion on Tatersale was only Lloyd's line of retreat. He hoped that Strayler's death would be taken as suicide or accident. In that case, according to his reasoning, the race would not be scratched, and he would get his Blue—and his £1,000. But if the police began sniffing about and suspecting murder, then Lloyd was all prepared with his bogus finger-prints and all the rest of the bag of tricks. He would lose his thousand, probably, but he would save his neck."

The Superintendent rubbed his cheek meditatively. "Do you mean," he asked, "that Lloyd only planted the spanner in the bushes *on Thursday afternoon,* when he saw you, Sir Francis Woodgate, Jevons, and all the rest, taking the affair seriously?"

"Very likely he did. I left the house before lunch, and for most of the afternoon the crew and their establishment had the house and garden to themselves, except for a few of Jevons's men. Perhaps Lloyd took an innocent stroll in the garden—why shouldn't he?—and planted his little piece of evidence only a few minutes before the Putney man dutifully found it. Or perhaps he bunged it into the bush the night before, as I thought at first. Of course, the finding of the spanner would pretty well dish his chances of the money, unless the police were so slow to act on it that the Boat Race could be rowed before anything was done. Lloyd, I expect, like most of us, valued his neck more highly than his £1,000, so he had to be prepared to risk the latter in order to make sure of the former."

"Humph!" commented the Superintendent. He lit a cigar, and spoke slowly between puffs. "But—my dear—fellow—why do you think—that the race would be rowed—even if Strayler—only died through accident—or—suicide? Wouldn't they call it off?"

"Well, as a matter of fact," MacNair admitted, "Lampson and Tatersale did agree to call it off, subject to the approval of the Oxford President, soon after the body was discovered. But there is no reason why the race should not have been merely postponed—at any rate, Lloyd would think so. There was a case, a great many years ago, I believe, when a member of the Cambridge crew was shot while he was cleaning his gun. The race was certainly held as usual that year; but in that case the tragedy occurred a month or two before the race. Now, in Lloyd's view—and you must make allowance for the warped mentality of a murderer—the Cambridge authorities would say: 'It wouldn't be fair to Oxford, and it wouldn't be fair to the new Blues, to scrap the race altogether. If Strayler had only broken his leg, we should have been obliged to carry on. The Oxford people will probably offer to scratch the fixture, but in fairness we can't accept that. We must agree to postpone the race, and hold it later, after a decent interval.' It would never occur to Lloyd that the race would be called off. As a matter of fact, there was an article in the *Daily Telephone* on Friday morning, before the inquest of course, written by an eminent Old Blue, in which he suggested that the race should be put off a month, or else that the two crews should agree to meet at Henley Regatta."

"In which case Lloyd's money would still be safe, assuming that he was given a place in the crew?"

"Exactly," answered MacNair.

"Well, there's something in that," said the Superintendent grudgingly. "What do you propose to do?"

"Well, I think we ought to release Tatersale. There was nothing against him except the finger-prints, and we know now how they got on the spanner."

"We think we know," amended the Superintendent.

"As you please. To me Dursfield's evidence is conclusive. And we could find no reasonable motive for Tatersale to murder Strayler, whereas we have very strong evidence of motive against Lloyd. We shall have to release Tatersale sooner or later, I am convinced; and the sooner we do it the less uproar there will be."

"Are you proposing to arrest Lloyd?" asked the Superintendent, a tone of anxiety in his voice. "For heaven's sake don't go and make another bloomer."

"I won't," said MacNair. "I'm not arresting any more Blues until I have a really good case. I shall watch brother Lloyd for a bit, and work quietly on the case until I'm sure of myself."

CHAPTER THIRTEEN

That afternoon, Mr. Bethell and Major Lampson were pacing slowly across one of the spacious lawns of Ranelingham, so deep in conversation that they were not aware of MacNair's approach until they heard his cheerful greeting.

"Well, sleuth-hound," said Lampson, "how's the case going?"

MacNair fell in step with them. "I have some good news for you," he said. "Robert Tatersale is to be released."

"By Jove! I am glad to hear that," cried Lampson, his face lighting up. "When?"

"As soon as the formalities can be complied with. Early to-morrow morning, probably."

"And who are you arresting in his place?" asked Bethell dryly.

"Nobody."

"Nobody?" echoed Bethell.

"No," said MacNair, "not a soul. I didn't want to arrest Tatersale, you know. It was forced on me by the verdict at the inquest. Since then I have been making further inquiries—I went down to Cambridge on Saturday." He did not mention the course of his investigations there. "I've gone into the case deeply, and the more I saw of it the more I realised that we hadn't the ghost of a case against Tatersale. So out he will come, with profuse apologies from me, and you I have no doubt will set the joy-bells ringing."

"But what about the case, then, if you are releasing Robert?" asked Lampson.

"Well, there isn't much more to be done about it. Sir Francis Woodgate and all the big noises at Scotland Yard are convinced that Strayler killed himself. So we're going to leave it at that."

"I said all along that it was preposterous to talk about murder," said Lampson. "But what about that ridiculous wilful murder verdict against Robert?"

"Oh, that won't count," answered MacNair. "Don't think that we're merely releasing him because we're afraid of not being able to get a verdict at the Old Bailey. It isn't a case of what we Scots call 'not proven.' We are now genuinely convinced that he had no hand in this crime—in fact, there was no crime," he added hastily, "except, perhaps, the crime of *felo de se.*" He did not relish the task of misleading his old friend, but he felt it necessary to lull the entire establishment at Ranelingham into the belief that the investigations had been dropped. Lloyd must have no idea that he was suspected; there must be no precipitate action this time.

"Then I suppose the crew can go home now?" said Lampson.

MacNair was disconcerted for a moment. This was not exactly what he wanted.

"Um . . . I don't know about that," he replied. "There will probably be some further legal formalities, you know. They may want a fresh inquest, or something of that sort. You know what lawyers are. I think it would be better to keep everybody at hand for a few days more, so that they can be called on to give fresh evidence if necessary. . . . I think they had better stay until the end of the week."

"That's going to be a nuisance," said Lampson. "They want to get away from all this as soon as they can."

"Of course they do. Are you living here with them, by the way?"

"Me? Good Lord, no. I'm at my club, the Senior University. Lewis and I are both stopping there. We came over this morning to have lunch with the crew."

"How are they? All merry and bright?"

"Fairly," said Bethell. "They haven't seen a reporter since they came here on Friday. One enterprising photographer was caught perched on the wall yesterday, but the policeman on duty soon had him out of that."

"I suppose Robert will be going home as soon as he gets out?" asked Lampson.

"I don't know," said MacNair. "Where is his home?"

"He lives somewhere down in Dorset, I believe."

"Does he? In that case, I'm afraid he will have to stay in London for a few days, until everything is finally settled. He might as well come here and live with the others."

"Mm—perhaps," said Lampson dubiously. "Do you think the Ranelingham authorities would like it—I mean, just out of prison, you know. . . ."

"Horace, you're a fool," snapped Bethell. "The boy mustn't be treated like a pariah. He hasn't done anything. There isn't a breath of suspicion against him."

"Exactly," echoed MacNair. "Let him come here. His friends will be glad to welcome him. It's a dreadful experience for a young fellow to be arrested on a charge like that. He mustn't be made to feel that he is resting under a stigma. He must be helped to forget all about it."

"All right. I certainly don't want to hurt the boy," said Lampson. "I'll see the secretary about it."

They turned their steps towards the club-house.

"By the way," said MacNair casually, "I hear that you two were up at the house on Putney Hill the other morning."

"Yes," said Lampson. "Nothing wrong in that, I hope?"

"Oh, no. Jevons, the D.D.I., told me."

"I don't know what a D. D. I. is," replied Lampson, "but if he was that bald-headed fellow with a face like a horse I should be inclined to call him by another set of initials. He got very high-and-mighty with us, and treated us as though he suspected us of meditating a smash and grab raid. We got so sick of him that we left."

"He seemed to be looking for something," said Bethell. "If he had spoken nicely to us, we should have shown him what we found in the garden. As it was, we just walked off."

"Oh? Did you find something?" asked MacNair, dissembling his interest. "What was it?"

"This," said Bethell, producing a small object from his pocket. "We found it at the foot of one of the bushes, partly covered over with earth. I don't suppose it's anything important."

MacNair took the object and glanced at it. It was a small wooden handle, of a slightly different pattern from the handle of the spanner. It was worn with use, and the hole for the tang of whatever tool it was intended for was chipped at the rim, as though it had been enlarged to receive some larger instrument.

"Thanks," he said, pocketing it. "I'll keep this, although I don't imagine it has any bearing on the case." Inwardly he was jubilant. This was the very handle of which he had surmised the existence, and was one more proof of the validity of his theory.

A club servant intercepted them as they entered the door of the building.

"Major Lampson," he said. "A gentleman has called to see you."

From a small sitting-room which opened off the entrance-hall in which they stood, there waddled into sight a strange personage. He was fully six feet in height, and so bulkily built that he seemed in danger of bursting out of the rusty black clothes, semi-clerical in cut, which he was wearing. His face was a great florid oval, fringed with a straggling undergrowth of whisker and furnished with little piggish eyes and a bulbous and suggestive nose. Altogether, MacNair thought, like the old caricatures of the President of the Transvaal Republic.

He advanced, swaying gently from side to side like a great ship, and extended a clammy hand.

"Major Lampson?" he rumbled unctuously. "Allow me to introduce myself. My name is Raikes—William Raikes. You are the coach of the Cambridge crew, are you not ? I am a Cambridge man myself—ah, but that was many, many years ago." He sighed.

"And what can I do for you?" said Lampson, somewhat impatiently.

"Happening to be in London, and learning that the Cambridge crew had taken up their abode here," the stranger went on, "I took the liberty of calling, to inquire about the poor lad who passed away. Has the—ah—funeral taken place yet?"

"He is being buried to-day," replied Lampson.

"In London—where?"

"No, not in London. A London funeral was out of the question. It would have attracted too much publicity. We made arrangements by wire with his father, and the body was sent to his home, at Borston in Yorkshire. For obvious reasons, you will understand, we had all these arrangements kept out of the papers."

"Dear me," sighed Mr. Raikes. "I wish I had known that. I live in Yorkshire myself, Major Lampson. I wish I had been able to attend the last sad rites. I knew poor Alan well. He was a pupil of mine—a good, charming boy. . . . His dear father is an old, old friend of mine. What a pity, what a pity!"

An oily tear made its appearance at the corner of his left eye, and coursed slowly down the valley at the side of his nose.

"The miscreant who cut short his life is in prison, I understand," he continued. "He is to be hanged, I suppose?"

Lampson motioned to the detective. "This is Inspector MacNair, who has charge of the case," he replied. "He can tell you more than I can."

The little eyes of Mr. Raikes travelled slowly over MacNair.

"A police officer! Really!" he exclaimed. "You have a strong case against the murderer?"

"I am afraid I am not at liberty to discuss the case," MacNair replied stiffly. "We are quite satisfied with the course of our investigations, I may say. There may, or may not be, developments in the case to-morrow. These you will doubtless be able to learn from the newspapers."

"Oh," said the big man, a trifle hurt. "You needn't be afraid to tell me anything. I am discretion itself. . . . Still, I must not attempt to seduce the police from their duty, I suppose. . . . Well, gentlemen, I need not trouble you further." He picked up his hat, a shapeless black felt, and prepared to depart. "I wish I could have attended the funeral, I wish I could have attended the funeral."

The three men watched him as he rolled ponderously down the drive.

"An odd old bird," commented MacNair when he was out of earshot.

"Some old fraud," said Lampson, with a contemptuous shrug. "I suppose he once met the Straylers somewhere, and considers himself a friend of the family."

"Or he may be the latest thing in reporters," suggested Bethell.

"I hardly think that," said MacNair. "He would ruin the reputation of any newspaper. But I wasn't giving anything away. He can jolly well wait for the news of Tatersale's release till he reads it to-morrow."

"Would you care to come in and see the crew?" asked Lampson. "They're all about somewhere."

"I don't think so, thanks. It would only upset them to see a rozzer prowling about the place. I really only came to tell you about Tatersale."

As he passed a wing of the building on his way out, a french window opened and a young man came out. "Good-bye, Tony old man," sounded the voice of Tom Scorby from within. "Awfully good of you to come."

MacNair at once recognised the pink-faced, fair-haired young man as Tony Bellison, the much-photographed Oxford President. He introduced himself, and the two engaged in conversation as they strolled towards the gate.

"So old Robert is cleared of suspicion, and you're going to let him out? Gosh, I'm pleased to hear that. Sickening business, you know, to have a chap had up for murder like that. It might muck up the Boat Race permanently. We all said, of course, that Alan did it himself. I mean, he was always a queer, nervous sort of chap, you know. Sort of silly ass kind of thing you might expect him to do. I don't want to speak unkindly of him, you know, but he *was* an odd fish."

"Did you know him well?"

"Oh, Lord, yes," replied Bellison. "I was at Eton with him, you know. Knew his people and all that kind of thing—at least his father. A rum old egg. Lost all his money somehow. It was all tied up with an entail or whatever the thing is, and nobody could touch it till Alan was of age. He was always talking about dodges to get money—old Strayler, you know—but I never paid any attention to them. It was too deep for me."

"You have stayed with the Straylers, then?"

"Yes, once, one summer, when Alan and I were at Eton. Dull sort of place, though. Up in Yorkshire. Nothing to do."

"Did Alan ever have a tutor, do you know?" asked MacNair.

"Tutor?" Tony Bellison looked puzzled. "Don't think so. . . . Wait a bit. Two years ago, before he went up to Cambridge, he went to some sort of a crammer, at Whitby, I think. He was a bit rocky, you know, where books were concerned, and he had to put in a bit of cramming before he got to Cambridge. The Little-Go, or some such silly name I think they call it."

"I see," said MacNair. "Do you know any of the others in the Cambridge crew at all well?"

"Some of them. Of course I know Robert fairly well. And Ramsey was at Eton, you know."

"Do you know Lloyd, the spare man?"

Bellison shook his head. "Only by sight, and that sort of thing."

They parted at the gate. Tony Bellison strode off in search of the nearest bus route; MacNair paced slowly on, fingering the wooden handle that lay in his overcoat pocket.

CHAPTER FOURTEEN

The two coaches, finding the club smoking-room empty, seated themselves in comfortable leather-lined arm-chairs before the fire and pulled out their pipes.

"I'm glad this miserable business is settled now," said Bethell, methodically teasing the tobacco from his pouch into his worn briar "I like your friend MacNair, but he has the policeman's mind. There is more rejoicing in Scotland Yard over one sinner who taps his fellow-man on the skull with a blunt instrument than over a cityful of peaceful citizens. How absurd to rush off and arrest Robert on such a charge!"

"Ridiculous," agreed Lampson. "Old Angus is well-meaning, but he never was strong in brains Why they put him in Scotland Yard I cant imagine. All that tommy-rot about finger-prints on a spanner!"

Bethell gave a start. "Good Lord!" he exclaimed. "I had forgotten the spanner. We never asked him about that."

"I expect he found some rational explanation of it. . . . By the way, I noticed that you didn't say anything to him about that paper you found."

"No, I didn't," said Bethell. "I was going to, but when he said that he had dropped his investigations I didn't see why I should. It would only create more bother. MacNair would only go rushing about the place like an excited puppy, suspecting everybody right and left. Anyway, I don't suppose it is anything of the slightest importance. I rather thought of keeping it, and trying my hand at unravelling it. A change from crosswords."

"Where did you find it, exactly? In the billiard-room, was it?"

"Yes; weren't you there?"

"I was out in the garden, you remember. It was just before that infernal policeman came nosing about."

"I found it in the fire-place," Bethell explained. "Somebody had crumpled it into a ball and pitched it into the fire, but it overshot the grate. The police should have spotted it for themselves. If they can't see things like that, it's their own lookout."

"Let's have another look at it."

Bethell pulled a crumpled piece of paper from his pocket and smoothed out its creases.

"Beats me," said Lampson, looking over his shoulder.

It was a sheet of cheap ruled paper, covered with a mass of undivided, unpunctuated figures:

```
2435453161552121711244824135231112911533615
4313527113312552717133125521114412332231812
2115513121311552475488352132403513516709121
1525144111172115113316311211233552154455136
3363115241244441533458811211511315131528935
6112112338765512441233523115451290763993314
4441211211545742316117117315242314231431352
3187112131642131511521522318431352112891315
2311544139867334423211222212331451244251444
4314515118890135152541544112431311112335653
5135121155131331311861113544570986243111213
1243111211345673513513452133413443111133124
3454133578121123135154454231423111113152124
3351351451245331311113154546092431112131543
1444423316345111133334153431528703151313312
3322353431521121314231711711315281265231543
5133335135152881882331131545412553173322311
1134531511244314413243187960001121134535135
1155423153544769823315231153371233553133121
3514496421335612152444135252354313528218812
2443135212155423153544541232314501121315415
4542511112437743151131211544997453122523163
1451121151121312451441155132331870623211315
5231425111431511314412334461185251243133114
4245144118091342313574231513152352215523143
5154243578453115524213357635135121155131701
5888441131523311154432152131154513433513518
9067112112333213431121316778221324431352118
1121151181211231254547425212335511131121315
4154411879066353115524413433513515234131352
7135445513322543167676723125454121524665215
12323144.
```

"It gives me a headache just to look at it," Lampson continued. "What the dickens is it? Looks like a collection of telephone numbers to me."

"I don't know what it is," said Bethell, "but I do hope it's a cryptogram. I always like cryptograms in books, but I have never met one in real life before."

"Cryptogram? What's that? Do you mean a secret code, or something? Who on earth would be writing cryptograms?" said Lampson irritably. "You're getting as bad as these policemen. Do you suggest that one of the crew is a Russian spy?"

"Or an Oxford spy," smiled Bethell. "That would be a good idea for a mystery story. The Cambridge Blue who was an Oxford secret agent in disguise."

"You don't think it has anything to do with—with Alan's death?"

"Oh, Lord no. How could it? Probably one of the crew has been amusing himself by concocting a cipher; trying to emulate something he read in a novel, very likely."

"Then why not ask them?" suggested the practical Lampson.

"Certainly not. I'm going to puzzle this out for myself. It will give me something to do between now and next Sunday's 'Torquemada.'"

"Anybody who can solve 'Torquemada' ought to be able to solve a little thing like this on his head," said Lampson. "I don't know how you do it. I can never solve anything except the children's puzzles myself."

"Well, let's have a look at this teaser," said Bethell, taking out a pencil and an old envelope. "The first question is, do we know who wrote this?"

Lampson peered at the paper. "It's hard to tell much about handwriting when you have no words, only a string of figures," he said. "It doesn't look much like any of the crew's handwriting to me."

Bethell nodded agreement. "I must find some way of looking at the writing of each of them. I don't know their hands well enough. . . . Now, what do you make of the cipher itself?"

"Nothing whatever," was the emphatic reply.

"Oh, come," said Bethell persuasively. "I want your opinion. Does anything strike you, anything at all?"

Lampson stared hard at the paper. "Um. . . . I should say there were a lot of ones in it. But perhaps it's only because they are more noticeable."

"Yes, you're right," said Bethell. "Lots of ones. . . . Lots of twos, threes, fours, and fives. Fewer of the other figures. And some groups seem to recur fairly often. 4231, for example. Also 4444."

"Perhaps each figure stands for a letter," Lampson suggested. "In that case, you find the most frequent figure and call it E, don't you? I don't know how it goes on after that."

122

"E-t-a-o-i-n-s-h-r-d-l-u-c-m-f-w-y-p, and so on," murmured Bethell. "Somebody once told me that that was why linotype operators occasionally break out into a frenzy of etaoin-shrdluing, but I forget just how he explained it. But I don't think that can be right in this case. You see, you find four fours, four threes, and four ones in a row several times. There's no English word in which one letter is repeated four times running."

"It might be Welsh. Llllany-something."

"If it's a Welsh love-letter written by our worthy spare man," said Bethell, "I shall give it up at once. But I don't think it's that. It might be one of these book ciphers, you know. The first figure refers to the page, the second to the line, the third to the word, in a particular book. If you haven't got the right book, you're absolutely dished."

"Yes. ..." Lampson was becoming interested. "But there's no sort of division. Take the beginning: '2435453,' and so on. How can you tell whether it's page 2, line 43, word 5, or page 24, line 3, or page 243 ..."

"Yes, yes," interrupted Bethell. "Don't go on ringing the changes. My head's in a whirl, as it is. I call it most inconsiderate of the compiler not to separate the letters, or even the words. I don't think it can be a book cipher, after all. It's probably something very simple, if only we knew the secret."

Lampson grunted sceptically. "If it's as complicated as it looks, it may be fool-proof, but it can hardly be a practical sort of cipher. By the time your spy had coded his message, and the blokes at the other end had decoded it, the war or whatever it was would be over."

"It must be something simple," said Bethell. "None of our fellows have the brains to concoct anything really deep. . . . Come on, now. Notice how comparatively few nines and noughts there are? I wonder what that means?"

"Perhaps they mark the ends of words, or sentences."

Bethell scratched his head. "No, I don't think it can be that. . . . Perhaps they indicate sums of money, or figures. . . ." He threw down his pencil with an impatient gesture. "I don't know what it means. I don't know what any of it means. Probably the infernal thing proves that Bacon wrote Shakespeare."

There was a sudden interruption of voices in the hall outside, followed by the slam of a door.

"I call you a rotten cad!" came the voice of a girl, shrill with passion. "How dare you suggest that Alan should have done such a thing to himself? How can you try to make love to me, when he isn't even in his grave yet? Beast!"

Bethell and Lampson looked at one another with raised eyebrows.

"Don't shout, Helen. There are people about." The two coaches recognised Tom Scorby's voice, low-pitched though it was.

"I will shout! I'll do what I damned well please!"—Bethell tck-tcked in disapproval, for he was a man of old-fashioned ideas—"I know what you are," stormed the girl. "*I believe you killed Alan yourself!*"

"For heaven's sake be quiet!" came the agitated voice of Scorby.

There was a click, suggestive of a small foot stamping upon the marble pavement.

"I won't be quiet! If you were half a man you'd take your medicine and be in prison now, instead of that other poor boy. Oh, it's odious!"

Another and louder slam followed; and presently the crunch of footsteps on gravel sounded outside. With one accord the two coaches stole to the window and looked out. They beheld a slim young girl, fashionably dressed; she might have been accounted beautiful, had it not been for her blazing eyes, her grimly shut mouth, and her face drained of colour. With a firm step she strode down the drive out of sight.

"A nice scene in a respectable club," commented Lampson.

They had scarcely regained their chairs when the door opened to admit Hugh Gawsell.

"Better tuck that paper away," murmured Lampson. Bethell hastily folded his "cryptogram" and placed it in his pocket. "Well, cox?"

Little Gawsell was obviously bursting with suppressed excitement. "Did you hear anything?" he asked.

"We certainly heard a slight disturbance in the hall," said Bethell. "Not a friend of yours, I hope?"

"Of mine? Lord, no," answered the coxswain, dropping into an armchair some four sizes too large for him and taking out a cigarette. "That was the girl. Alan's girl, you know."

"No, I don't know. How should I know?" Bethell said testily.

"Oh, don't you? Her name's Helen something-or-other. She was engaged to Tom last year. Then she met Alan at Henley, or it may have been May Week, and she promptly fell in love with him instead. They were practically engaged—it was to have been announced after the Boat Race, I think. Old Tom was fearfully shirty about it. That's why he wouldn't speak to Alan, you know. Alan always had her photograph about with him in his pocket. Used to take it out and make eyes at it when he thought nobody was looking."

"What did she come here for?" inquired Lampson.

"She came to see Tom—I don't know why. Perhaps she wanted to be on with the old love."

"Did she come here alone?" Bethell was mildly scandalised.

"Of course. Why not?"

"The modern girl will do anything," said Lampson.

"Well—you heard what she was shouting?" Gawsell continued. "I don't know what they said at first. They were in the drawing-room. I imagine Tom tried to tell her that Alan killed himself, and she was indignant at the idea that anybody who was engaged to her should want to commit suicide. But Tom never was tactful."

"Did all the rest of the crew hear this ?"

"No, I don't think any of them did. They are all out in the grounds somewhere."

"All except you, eh?" said Lampson. "Trust you to be flapping your ears about when anything Is happening."

Gawsell, like most coxswains, was impervious to insult. Adopting an air of mystery, he leaned forward and asked:

"Do you think there is anything in what she said?"

"What do you mean?" said Bethell.

"I mean—that Tom killed Alan."

Bethell and Lampson groaned simultaneously.

"That Scotland Yard man dropped me a hint the other day——"

"I wish he had dropped a brick on you," said Lampson savagely.

CHAPTER FIFTEEN

"Could Mr. Strayler see you for a few moments, sir?"

MacNair nearly dropped the telephone in his astonishment.

"Mr. Strayler?" he repeated stupidly.

"Yes, sir," said the voice at the other end of the wire. "Mr. Bartley Strayler. He wishes to see you about the Strayler murder, sir."

"Send him up."

A few minutes later the visitor made his appearance ; a frail, bent man, who walked slowly and painfully with the aid of a stick. His face, partly concealed by an ill-kept grey beard, was lined and shrunken. A network of tiny purple veins ran this way and that across the pale, delicate skin. MacNair had never seen Alan Strayler in life; he strove to catch some resemblance between this old man and the photographs he had seen of the fair-haired, finely-featured youth, but could see none, unless it were some fleeting look in the sunken eyes into which he gazed.

He gently assisted the old man to his most comfortable chair, and seated himself at his desk, facing him.

"You wished to see me, Mr. Strayler?" he asked. "I am the officer in charge of—of the investigations into Alan Strayler's death."

"My son," said the old man. His voice was weak and tired. "I could not come to London sooner. I am a sick man, Inspector. The journey last night was almost too much for me."

He passed a hand over his brow.

"My son was buried yesterday," he continued. "I—I felt that I could not rest until I learned the secret of his death. The police inspector from York who came to see me was very kind, but of course he could tell me nothing. Tell me—why should this young man, a complete stranger to me, wish to hurt Alan?"

There was a pathetic bewilderment in his voice that touched MacNair deeply.

"You may rest assured that Robert Tatersale never harmed your son," he said. "He was released from prison this morning."

"Then—then what happened?"

"We now know the identity of the real criminal, Mr. Strayler," answered MacNair. "We are building up our case against him, and we can lay our hands on him at any time."

"But why . . . why did he do it?"

"Not from any motive of hatred or jealousy towards your son. It was, I am afraid, a despicable, cold-blooded crime, for the sake of gaining money. The criminal will receive the punishment he deserves."

"Money?" repeated the old man. "Not Alan's money? He couldn't touch Alan's money."

"Did your son possess money?" MacNair asked. "You will forgive me, but I understood . . ."

The old man made a weary gesture. "You have heard of my circumstances, perhaps. I have been a poor father, I am afraid. I had money once, but—" He waved his hand again. "There is an estate, a good estate for these hard times. It is—I should say, was—entailed for Alan's benefit. I could not touch the capital; that was fortunate, perhaps. Money never remained long in my hands. There was an oil well in Texas—a gold mine, I forget where." He sighed.

MacNair was not greatly interested, but he listened courteously.

"Some years ago," Mr. Strayler went on, "I mortgaged my interest in the estate, for £55,500. It was a foolish thing to do, perhaps, but I needed the money. Then—I was unable to pay the interest, and the insurance company foreclosed. My only source of income had passed into the hands of strangers. My only hope was to persuade Alan to break the entail when he came of age."

"When would that have been?" asked MacNair.

"Not until next year. He is—he was barely twenty when he died."

"I met a young man named Bellison yesterday," said MacNair. "He told me that he knew you."

"Tony Bellison—I remember him. A charming young fellow, and a great friend of Alan's. He is in the Oxford boat now, is he not?"

"He told me also," MacNair continued, "that you—er—had some plan, for getting back this money."

"Not the mortgage money," said the old man. "When Bellison came to us, three or four years ago, there had been no question of the company's foreclosing. It must have been that wretched gold mine he heard me speak about. But I did have a scheme about the mortgage," he added.

"Really?" said MacNair absently.

"I have an old friend, Mr. Raikes. He acted as tutor to my son just before he went up to Cambridge. Raikes was once a Fellow at Cambridge himself—a very brilliant man. But he gave up his University career, and settled at Whitby. Two years ago, as I say, Alan went to him as a pupil, and I also visited him at Whitby for a fortnight. Raikes was very kind, very kind indeed. I am sorry to say that I have never been able to pay him for Alan's tutoring, nor even for our board and lodging. But Raikes is such a kind fellow—he has never pressed me for payment."

"And did Raikes have anything to do with the scheme you mentioned?" MacNair was at last becoming interested.

"Oh, yes. It was his idea. He proposed to buy my interest in the estate from the insurance company. Of course, that would have been quite a good investment for him. Unfortunately, he did not possess enough money; but he told me that he could probably borrow it, on the security of the interest he proposed to buy."

"But how would you have profited by this transaction, Mr. Strayler?"

"Well, you see," the old man explained, " Raikes's idea was to per-suade Alan to break the entail, when he came of age. Raikes is very clever, Inspector. I don't know how he thinks of these things. If Alan broke the entail, it was estimated that the freehold alone could be sold for over ,£200,000. I think the exact figure was ,£202,500. When the mortgage had been paid off, and various legal expenses settled, quite a large sum of money would remain. I think Raikes put it at £133,000."

"And who would get the money?" asked MacNair.

"Alan of course would get most of it. Raikes proposed to let Alan have £100,000 as his share, and we agreed to divide the remainder between ourselves."

"A very nice scheme," commented MacNair. "I take it, though, that it did not go through?"

"Alas, no," said the old man sadly. "You see, it was necessary for my life to be insured; and no insurance company would touch me. They said I was a very bad life. . . . And now Alan is gone, and here am I."

"Was your son's life insured?"

The old man looked puzzled. "No," he replied. "I don't think it could have been. He would have told me about it. And who could he leave his money to but me? I should have heard of it by now."

"I see," said MacNair. "And—did Raikes propose any other schemes after the first one fell through?"

"No. I have not seen him for some time. Alan visited him at Whitby last summer, but I did not go."

"Has Raikes a family, Mr. Strayler?"

"Not that I know of. He is unmarried, or so he has always led me to believe."

"Have you ever known, or heard of, a young man named Owen Lloyd?"

"Never, to my knowledge."

MacNair rose. "Thank you very much for coming, Mr. Strayler," he said. "Let me once more assure you that the brutal murder of your son will not go unpunished."

When his visitor had thanked him and departed, MacNair wrote two telegrams. The replies came a few hours later.

The first was from the Chief Constable's office at Cambridge:

"William Raikes was undergraduate St. Faith's College. First class mathematical tripos 1893, Fellow of St. Faith's 1895. Painful scene in 1899. Intoxicated in college chapel, asked resign Fellowship. Present address unknown."

The second was from Whitby, and ran:

"William Raikes came here about 1905, took house 67 Bardsleigh Road. Takes pupils as private tutor or crammer. No other source of livelihood known. Nothing known against him."

MacNair studied the two telegrams, and frowned. "Now, does Lloyd fit into this—or doesn't he?" he murmured.

CHAPTER SIXTEEN

Robert Tatersale was released from Brixton Prison, whither he had been sent on remand, early that morning. He was given a hearty welcome by his crew-mates, and even the most tactless among them forebore from references to skilly, oakum-picking and kindred topics.

"What I want to know," said Robert, "is, what about it?"

It was after lunch, and the crew were stretched lazily in arm-chairs in the smoking-room.

"You mean, about—?" Bonzo Kirkpatrick thought it safer to end his sentence with an aposiopesis.

"Yes, that," said Robert. "I mean, what about it? They told me they had dropped the case against me, but they didn't say what they were going to do next. And they say we must all stay here until about the end of the week. What's the idea of that?"

"Dunno," said Bonzo, lazily indifferent. "It's a good spot. Suits me all right."

"It may suit a great lump of suet like you, but I want to get away from London, and forget all this. . . . What are these detectives doing? Are they going to arrest some other poor beggar?"

"Ask cox," said Tom Scorby. "He's our great detective expert."

"He is, is he?" Robert cocked an eye at him. "Well, Sherlock, what's the next move?"

Hugh Gawsell looked wise. "They say they have dropped the case altogether, and that they have decided it was suicide or accident," he said. "But I know better."

"In-deed," exclaimed Scorby. "And what do you know, you little pip-squeak?"

Gawsell contented himself with a melodramatic "Aha!"

"I wish somebody would drown that kid," said Salvago disgustedly. "He is perfectly intolerable. The only thing he hasn't done yet is to crawl about the floor with a magnifying glass, putting cigarette-ash in little envelopes and measuring footprints."

"I have my eye on somebody," Gawsell said solemnly. "Important developments may be expected——"

A well-aimed cushion caught him in the wind.

"You didn't expect that one," said Bonzo, with a grin.

Later in the day, when the shadows of a gloomy, rain-swept afternoon had fallen, Hugh Gawsell stole into the smoking-room. The two coaches, who had again visited the crew that afternoon, in order to welcome Robert Tatersale, were seated by the fire in the otherwise empty room.

"Thought I should find you here," said the coxswain. "I've got something for you."

"Can't you leave us in peace, cox?" grunted Lampson, who was half asleep. "What is it?"

Gawsell produced a book, which Bethell took and examined lazily. It was a red-backed novel, bearing the label of the Putney branch of Brown's library.

"Well, what about it?"

"I found it lying about this morning," said Gawsell. "It should have been taken back to Brown's with the other books, but I suppose it got overlooked, and taken on here with our other stuff from the Putney Hill house."

"Yes, but what's peculiar about it?"

"Look inside the back cover."

Bethell looked. "There's nothing there."

"Yes, there is," maintained Gawsell. "Somebody wrote something on the inside of the cover in pencil, and then rubbed it out. But if you hold it to the light you can just make it out."

With a grumble, Bethell switched on a small reading-lamp and examined the book carefully. This is what he read, faintly marked in capital letters:

T I O J A
H C W M Z
E K N P Y
Q B F S D
U R X L G

"And what is this supposed to be, cox?" he asked.

"I don't know. I thought you might be interested in it."

Major Lampson leaned over Bethell's shoulder. "The first word looks like Spanish," he remarked. "The second might be Polish or Russian or almost anything, and the rest is just nonsense. It isn't part of a cross-word puzzle, is it?"

"Of course not," snapped Bethell. "Don't you know what a crossword looks like? . . . Wait a bit. . . . If you read downwards, it starts to spell something. 'The quick brown,' and then it goes off into gibberish, except for the word 'lazy.'"

"I see what it is!" cried Gawsell suddenly. " 'The quick brown fox jumps over the lazy dog.' Only the letters that repeat are left out, and there doesn't seem to be a 'v' anywhere. It's the thing typists write for practice, or to test their machines. Like 'Now is the time for all good men to come to the aid of the party,' and 'Pack my bag with six dozen liquor jugs.'"

"What *is* he talking about?" Lampson complained.

"But why do you bring us this, cox?" said Bethell. "Why shouldn't somebody scribble about quick brown foxes in the back of a book?"

The coxswain's face fell. "I thought it might be important. I thought it might be a clue, or something."

"Another cryptogram, I suppose?" Lampson snorted.

"Is there a cryptogram?" asked Gawsell with interest.

"No, there isn't," Bethell said quickly. "Horace and I had been talking about the Bacon-Shakespeare theory. Who was reading this book?"

"Oh, everybody, I expect," Gawsell answered. "It's been lying about for weeks."

"You don't know whose writing this is?"

"I don't think you can tell, really. Nearly everybody writes block capitals the same way. Besides, it's so faint that you can only just make it out."

Bethell closed the book and laid it on a table. "Ah, well, I don't imagine it is anything of the slightest importance."

He sank back into his chair, and took up the evening paper he had been reading. It was clear that he had no wish for further conversation with the coxswain. As for Major Lampson, his eyes were frankly shut, and his breathing was becoming stertorous.

Undeterred, Gawsell took the best chair he could find and drew it up to the fire. He had manifestly no intention of going away.

"Whatever he may have told you, that fellow MacNair hasn't dropped the case, you know," he began.

Bethell lowered his newspaper. "Eh? What's that?"

"Not a bit of it," said the coxswain with relish. "He's going for a murderer—and it isn't Robert this time."

The curtains by the half-opened window stirred slightly, as though moved by a passing breeze.

"What on earth is your trouble now?" asked Bethell irritably.

"He spoke to me about a book called *The Rasp* the other day. Asked me who had been reading it, and so forth. I saw something was up, so I got hold of the book and read it. I tell you, Lewis, that book gives the whole show away." He outlined the plot of the novel and its application to Alan Strayler's death, in much the same way as that in which MacNair had explained it to the Superintendent three days before.

"He mentioned Lloyd particularly in connexion with it," he concluded. "At least, only Lloyd's name was mentioned. But I suspect that he only brought him up to put me off. I fancy he's really after somebody else!"

"Who?" Bethell was becoming interested in spite of himself.

"I don't know, but I have my ideas," said Gawsell, wagging his head sagely.

"Tom, do you mean?"

"Um . . . Tom perhaps. Yes, he is a possibility. You remember what that girl said yesterday There's a good motive there: Tom's girl——"

"Tom's fiancee, please!" murmured Bethell.

"All right, his fiancee. She jilts him, and gets engaged to Alan. Tom was awfully fed about it, you know. So Tom in revenge kills Alan."

"Just like an Italian opera," commented Bethell. "Cox, don't be so absurd."

"Well, you were the one who brought Tom up. I was thinking of some-body else. . . . Selfridge's."

Lampson awoke from his doze with a start. "Selfridge's? Salvago?" he muttered. "What about him?"

"Cox was just telling me a fairy-tale, to the effect that Salvago killed Alan, for some unexplained reason," said Bethell.

"It's not unexplained," said Gawsell. "I call it very likely. The very night it happened, he said he wouldn't mind a nice quiet murder on a night like that, and he offered to slit Owen Lloyd's throat for him."

"But that's nothing," objected Bethell. "Anybody might say that."

"Ah, but they wouldn't mean it. And Salvago would. He's got the Latin temperament, you know. They kill people for twopence in Italy. And you remember about his mother, don't you?"

"No. What did she do?" Lampson asked.

"It was in the papers a couple of years ago, when he was a fresher. It happened at Monte Carlo, or Nice, or one of those places. She took a revolver and had three or four pot-shots at her husband, because he wouldn't pay a dressmaker's bill. That's the sort of family they are."

"Did she kill him?"

"She never even hit him. The next day the judge reconciled them, and they wept on each other's shoulders and had a big dinner to celebrate it. There was a lot about it in a French paper. A bloke in our college who was in France at the time, and who knew Selfridge's, brought it back and showed it to me. But it just shows you, doesn't it ? I mean, if his ma would do a thing like that, he might easily kill Alan just because he was sick and tired of him, as he certainly was."

"I don't think he would," said Bethell. "He's half English, isn't he?"

"Yes, but it's his mother who's English, and she's the one who did the shooting," said Gawsell. "And he's a Socialist, you know. On the Continent Socialists are pretty dangerous birds, practically Bolsheviks. He was very sore with everybody the day before it happened; he was annoyed about that record, as I think I told you."

"What was wrong with it?" growled Lampson. "Perfectly good record."

"Oh, it was all right," Gawsell replied hastily. "But he didn't like it."

"But that's no reason for killing anybody," said Bethell. "Do shut up, cox. You give me a pain."

Gawsell relapsed into brooding silence, his chin propped on his fists. A few minutes later, when Lampson had once more dropped into a doze, he suddenly smote his palms together.

"I've got it!" he exclaimed.

"Shut up, cox!" roared the exasperated Lampson.

"I have, really. I see the whole thing now. I see how that *Rasp* story fits in. Oh, it's clever, beastly clever!"

Major Lampson rose from his chair and pointed to the door.

"If you don't clear out, cox, there will be another and particularly gory murder in five minutes' time. Now then, out you go!"

Gawsell lingered no more, but strode to the door with as much dignity as he could muster. Again the curtain moved slightly, and there was a faint sound, as of a stealthy foot treading lightly upon gravel.

"Horace, don't go to sleep. I want to talk to you," said Bethell, when the coxswain had gone. "Do you think there is anything at all in what he was saying?"

"Who? That nasty little cox?"

"Yes. Do you think that MacNair was—um— leading us up the garden, when he told us that the case was dropped?"

"No, of course he wasn't," said Lampson testily. "Angus has been perfectly frank with me all along. If he says the case is dropped, he means it."

"Well, that may be so," said Bethell, sucking his pipe reflectively. "But I am not quite satisfied about the business. Frankly, I don't like the atmosphere. I've never had a crew like this before."

"You don't believe all that rot of cox's about Salvago, do you?"

"No, I couldn't quite swallow that. But why is Gawsell continually trying to cast suspicion on other people—first Lloyd, then Tom Scorby, then Salvago?"

Lampson sat up. "Do you think he—knows anything about Alan's death?" he asked sharply.

"I have an idea that he does," Bethell replied quietly. "No ordinary young man, who had nothing to hide, would keep on going out of his way to suggest that undergraduate friends of his were murderers. It simply doesn't happen. I have a shrewd suspicion that our Mr. Gawsell is in a blue funk about something, and is trying to get one of his little chums into the mess that is rightly his. Now that Robert has been cleared, you see, anybody might be arrested next . . . and Gawsell may be afraid that he himself is for it."

"You're getting as bad as cox," grumbled Lampson. "How could he have had anything to do with Alan's death? He's such a little shrimp."

"Little shrimp he may be, but I think you can make out a stronger case against him than against any one else. In the first place, he has the right sort of character. What he was saying about Salvago's Latin temperament and so forth was all bosh. An excitable fellow like Salvago might stick a knife into his enemy in hot blood; he would never plan in advance a carefully constructed scientific crime like this. But that's just what Gawsell would be likely to do. He is a medical student, remember. He spends his days poking about into dead bodies, in some revolting laboratory to which I have heard him allude as 'meaters.' To him and his like, there is nothing terrifying, nothing even repugnant, about a corpse. They handle them daily. Human life can have no sanctity to them. To an experienced doctor, yes; but not to the callous fledglings of the medical school.

"Again," Bethell continued, "do you remember what MacNair said the other day? He taxed Gawsell with having boasted that with some medical or jiu-jitsu trick he could overpower a bigger man than himself. I remember treating that lightly at the time, but I have been thinking about it since. Gawsell could easily have knocked Alan out by some such trick, taking him unawares, and have added the tap on the head with the spanner to confuse the investigations."

"He would hardly make a boast like that, if he were planning to kill somebody the same night," Lampson objected.

"It may have slipped out accidentally. Or—he may have said it in the knowledge that somebody would make the objection you have just raised."

Lampson shook his head. "That's too deep for me," he murmured. "But what about all this stuff he was telling us about some novel?"

"I'm not quite clear about that," said Bethell. "I don't think, myself, that this novel had anything to do with it at all. He probably suggested it to MacNair as a blind, and MacNair swallowed it. Or he and MacNair may never have talked about it at all. I don't know. I rather fancy that he used some other dodge altogether. Perhaps the spanner which Robert handled got into the bushes in some quite innocent way, which Robert was afraid to speak about when he was arrested. I should have kept mum about it myself, I suppose, had I been in his position, although I know that it would be a foolish thing to do.

"Then, when Gawsell heard about this precious spanner, he concocted this cock-and-bull tale about this novel, *The Rasp,* and suggested it to MacNair and then to us. Either we should swallow it, and suspect Salvago or some other person, or else we should say 'how absurd!' and never dream of suspecting Gawsell of anything worse than an inventive imagination. Remember, by the way, that he has rather sharper wits than most of the others; he is very keen on detective stories, and knows all the tricks of the trade."

"And what about your cryptogram?" asked Lampson. "Did he write it?"

Bethell gave a start. "Good Lord!" he exclaimed. "Do you know, I had quite forgotten about the cryptogram for the moment."

He pulled the paper from his pocket and looked at it. "Yes, our little friend Gawsell might have written it, although it doesn't look like his hand."

"I can explain that," said Lampson suddenly. "I wonder I never thought of it before. Did you realise that cox adds forgery to his other accomplishments?"

"Forgery?"

"Yes, rather. I found him one day hard at work writing names in a pile of autograph books. I asked him what he was doing, and he explained that the crew had so many autograph books sent them that they couldn't keep up with the rush. So he taught himself to imitate all their signatures, and there he was filling up one album after another."

"I shall keep my cheque book locked up when he's about," said Bethell.

"I saw some of his efforts," Lampson went on, "and they were quite creditable. Nothing would have been easier for him than to write that puzzle of yours in a disguised hand—it is all figures, and figures don't show much individuality anyway—and leave it about for the police to find."

"You mean that it's a spoof? You are getting quite bright, Horace. Then no doubt the quick brown fox that he showed us just now is also of his own manufacture."

"It probably is. That was a pretty thin story he told. . . . Do you suppose the quick brown fox has any connexion with the other thing?"

Bethell opened the book and laid it on the table beside the paper.

"Hmm. ... If they are both cox's invention, the one is probably the key to the other. I wish I knew something about cryptograms. You haven't any fresh ideas, have you?"

"Not one," said Lampson. "It might be double Dutch as far as I'm concerned."

Bethell puzzled over the cryptogram for a few minutes, then put it aside with a sigh.

"I'm beginning to think we ought to show this to MacNair, and tell him our suspicions," he said.

"Perhaps you're right," Lampson agreed.

Hugh Gawsell nimbly mounted the broad stairs of the club-house, and made his way along the ill-lit and twisting corridor that led to his bedroom. He did not see the dark form that lurked in the shadows, nor the arm that was lifted to strike.

CHAPTER SEVENTEEN

Late that afternoon, an agitated official of the Meteor Insurance Company visited Scotland Yard, and, having explained his business, was sent to Inspector MacNair's room. Without preamble, he plunged at once into his story.

"In August of last year," he said, "Mr. Alan Strayler insured his life with us, through our York branch." MacNair was instantly alert. "He was insured for £20,000 in all—there were two proposal forms, of £10,000 each. Strayler was found to be an excellent life; and the first annual premiums, of £150 each, were paid, on August 14th."

"One moment," said MacNair. "The address was The Manor, Borston, Yorkshire, was it not ? You are referring to the Alan Strayler who died last week at Putney?"

"Oh yes, it was that Strayler right enough," said his visitor. He consulted his memoranda. "The permanent address was certainly Borston; but his temporary address, at the time of taking out the policy, was 67, Bardsleigh Road, Whitby. On August 17th, Strayler wrote to our York branch, instructing them that in the event of his death the insurance money was to be paid to William Raikes, M.A., of the address in Whitby which I just gave you."

MacNair gave a start. "But surely—" he began.

"One moment." The other held up a hand. "This morning our York branch received a letter from Mr. Raikes, asking for the payment of the money."

"Of all the colossal cheek!" said MacNair.

"Exactly. Strayler was, at the time of his death, a minor; and an assignment by a minor is not good in law. Our people in York have, I am afraid, acted rather carelessly. They should at once have written to Strayler to point this out. But, having of course no idea that he would die so soon, they took no action. They have now wired to us for instructions."

"Where did Raikes write from—Whitby?" asked MacNair. "He was certainly in London yesterday, for I saw him."

"I think I can answer that," said the official. "Here is the telegram from York: '. . . Letter written on plain note-paper, headed "as from 67, Bardsleigh Road, Whitby, April 13th." Postmark, London, E.C.4.' "

"Smart work," commented MacNair. "Not everybody would have thought to send all that information."

The official smiled. "I fancy our York manager has the wind up rather. He should have gone to the police as soon as he heard of Strayler's death."

"Had you no record, then, of this transaction at your London head-quarters?"

"Yes, of course we must have," the other replied. "But we do such a lot of this class of business that I don't suppose any one at our London office noticed the name of Strayler among the lists of our clients."

A sudden thought struck the detective.

"Was it by any chance your firm that held a mortgage on Mr. Bartley Strayler's estate, or rather his life interest in it?" he inquired.

The official pondered for a moment. "I don't think so. That is rather outside our line. But I can make inquiries."

"I wish you would," said MacNair. "And I should very much like to have another chat with Mr. Raikes. He begins to interest me, although I hardly see how he can have had any hand in Strayler's murder."

"Murder!" exclaimed the startled official. "I understood that you had come to the conclusion that his death was due to suicide. That is why we were worried about the insurance."

"Since you have been good enough to come to us with this informa-tion," replied MacNair in confidential tones, "I don't mind giving you a little in exchange. We still believe it to be a case of murder. We know who did it, and we hope to make an arrest very shortly. I can't tell you who it is, but the case against him has nothing to do with this insurance policy. . . . Nevertheless, the more I think of it the more I feel a strong desire to renew my acquaintance with William Raikes, M.A."

When the insurance official had left, MacNair despatched another wire to the police at Whitby. At the same time, he issued an all-stations message, giving a full description of the wanted man.

He was completing this task when his telephone rang. It was Jevons; and his message caused MacNair to hurry out of the building and to dash to Ranelingham in a taxi.

He was met by Jevons under the tall portico of the club.

"Well?" he asked. "Have you made an arrest? Where's the body?"

"Body? He's not a body yet. Bit of luck for him that he isn't. As proper a bit of cosh-work as ever I saw," replied Jevons. "That Dr. Trunch got here before I did, and had him taken to a nursing-home in Fulham."

"Yes," said MacNair impatiently, "but who attacked him? Have you arrested anybody?"

"How can you arrest anybody, when any one of the lot might have done it?" said Jevons, in aggrieved tones. "I never met such a bunch of young garrotters. First tying people up and chucking them into baths, and now bashing each other's heads in! Call themselves Cambridge College! If they were the Borstal rowing crew they'd be better behaved!"

"What was it done with?"

"This." Jevons produced a twelve-inch length of heavy garden hose. "That's the right stuff. Wraps itself round your skull and concusses you no end. And no finger-prints this time. He used a glove, I expect, or rubbed the marks off afterwards."

"Did he speak at all?"

"Don't think so."

"Well, you might ring up the nursing-home and ask after him," said MacNair. "I see Major Lampson inside—I'll find out what he has to say."

Lampson and Bethell were pacing nervously up and down the spacious entrance hall. Several of the crew were standing about in twos and threes, with anxiety and bewilderment written on their faces. MacNair greeted the two coaches, and led them aside.

"What on earth has been happening now?" he asked, in a low voice. "I couldn't get much out of Jevons."

"It's Gawsell this time," answered Lampson.

"Yes, I knew that much. How did it happen?"

"He was struck down outside his bedroom, when he went up to change for dinner. Nobody saw it happen. Here's Tom—he can tell you about it."

Tom Scorby had gone to his room, which was near the coxswain's, to dress for dinner, at about a quarter to seven, he told MacNair. Most of the others had gone upstairs at the same time. About ten minutes later he heard a low cry, and immediately afterwards the sound of a fall. At the time he imagined that some of the crew were ragging in the passage outside. Later, hearing no more noise, his curiosity prompted him to look out. He did so, and found Gawsell lying unconscious a few yards up the passage, with the length of rubber hose beside him. He at once gave the alarm, and Gawsell was carried into his own bedroom, while Dr. Trunch was telephoned for.

"The rest of the crew—were they all upstairs ?" asked MacNair.

"Yes, I think so," answered the burly oarsman. "At least, I think I saw everybody after I gave the alarm. Most of the chaps were half-way through dressing, but they all ran out of their rooms to see what was going on."

"I see," murmured MacNair. His eye roved round the room until it lit on the lean figure of Owen Lloyd, who was leaning against a pillar and jerkily puffing at a cigarette. He had almost made up his mind to go over to him when he heard the voice of Bethell at his elbow.

"A dreadful thing, this," said the coach in a low tone. "And do you know, just before it happened Horace Lampson and I had made up our minds that Gawsell was the murderer of Alan."

"What made you think that?" asked MacNair sharply.

"Oh, it's too absurd now," said Bethell, with a wry smile. "We found a paper, and . . . Come into the smoking-room and we can talk about it."

He led the way, followed by MacNair and Lampson. When the door was shut, he took the cryptogram from his pocket.

"I have a confession to make," he said, a little awkwardly. "The fact is, that handle wasn't the only thing we found at Putney Hill." He went on to relate how the paper was found.

MacNair was annoyed, and said as much.

"You'll excuse my saying so, but amateur sleuths give me a pain," he said angrily. "We have men at Scotland Yard who could decipher a thing like that on their heads—men who were doing that sort of work all through the war. Do you realise that you have made yourself an accessory after the fact?"

"I'm dreadfully sorry," said Bethell humbly. "I thought you had dropped the case. There was another thing, by the way, that cox showed us—it may have something to do with the cipher. I left it in here."

He crossed the room, and stopped short as he beheld the small table that stood by the fire-place. The library novel was no longer there.

"I'll swear it was there an hour ago," he muttered. A careful search of the room revealed no trace of the missing book.

"Perhaps somebody's taken it to the reading-room," he said finally. "I'll look there."

Followed by the two others, he crossed the hall and entered a large, comfortable room, furnished with capacious chairs and large tables on which the daily and evening papers were laid out in orderly rows. Bethell rapidly scanned the room.

"Doesn't seem to be here," he said.

"There are some books here," called MacNair from one corner of the room. "What sort of book was it?"

Bethell walked to the little book-case. "No, these are only the crew's own books," he said, taking out a volume idly. "Nothing——"

The book he held fell to the floor with a crash.

"What's the matter?" asked MacNair, turning quickly. Bethell was standing motionless, his eyes staring as though he beheld a vision.

"Futhark," he muttered.

"What? What's he saying?" exclaimed Lampson.

"Futhark," said Bethell once more. His eyes were now gleaming with excitement as he turned to his two companions. "Now I'm going to decipher that document."

"What about your quick brown fox?" asked Lampson.

"I think I can remember how it was arranged. Now, please leave me alone for a bit, with a pencil and some paper."

MacNair hesitated. "It would be much quicker if I sent it to Scotland Yard," he demurred.

"No, no," pleaded Bethell. "I can solve it myself now. What's more, *I know who wrote it.*"

"Who?"

"Never mind. I'll tell you when I have deciphered it."

As MacNair stepped out into the hall Jevons came up to him.

"I got through to the nursing-home, sir," he reported. "He's got very bad concussion, and he's still unconscious."

MacNair swore softly.

"There was another message for you, from Scotland Yard," Jevons went on. "The Whitby police have wired to say that Raikes is believed to have left Whitby on Saturday morning. He told his servant he was going to London and expected to be back on Tuesday—that's to-day."

"No other messages?"

"No, sir."

MacNair paced up and down the hall. Should he arrest Lloyd at once? No, Lloyd was safe enough. He could lay his hands on him at any moment. It would be better, perhaps, to see what Bethell made of the cryptogram.

A club servant interrupted his meditations to summon him to the telephone.

The message was from Scotland Yard. "Information has just come in," said a voice, "that a man answering your description took a room on

Saturday evening at the Coburg Hotel in Peters-field Street, near King's Cross. He gave his name as William Raikes. He left the hotel this morning.

"Do they know where he went?"

"No. He didn't take a taxi. He walked out of the hotel, carrying his suitcase."

"Very likely he doesn't yet know he's wanted," said MacNair. "He may be going back to Whitby to-night. There's a night train from King's Cross that stops at York, isn't there? Find out if that train is any good for Whitby, and have the station watched. Better have all the stations watched as well—he may be going to bolt."

A quarter of an hour later, the door of the reading-room opened and Bethell appeared, his spectacles slightly askew, a broad smile of satisfaction on his face.

"Come in," he said, "I have something to show you."

"Quick work," said MacNair, as he and Lampson followed him into the room.

"It was simple enough, once I got the clue," Bethell said modestly. "Without the quick brown fox, though, I couldn't have done it. Perhaps your Yard experts might, but it would have been beyond me."

The table at which he had been working was littered with papers. He selected one, and seated himself.

"Now listen to this."

"My dear nephew, (he read.)

"It is more than a fortnight since I have heard from you. I trust that nothing has gone amiss, and that everything is in readiness. It had better be before the Boat Race, for the reasons which we discussed at our last meeting. You have not told me the method you propose to employ. It would be better if you did not tell me. The less we put on paper, even in cipher, the better. I rely on your intelligence to devise some safe method. You always were an ingenious boy. I am sorry for him, for I always liked the lad, but if fate has decreed that he must go, we, who are but fate's instruments, must obey. Be very careful, my dear boy. You have a stern task ahead of you. Think of the comfort that it will bring to the last years of

Your poor old uncle,
William Raikes."

"Well, I'll be ... I don't know *what* I'll be," gasped Lampson, when Bethell had finished. "The sanctimonious old hound! Who's the nephew?"

"I think I know," Bethell answered, "but I can't be sure, of course. When I told you I knew who wrote this letter, I was wrong. I had no idea that this fellow Raikes had anything to do with it."

"Well, tell us what you suspect," said MacNair impatiently.

"I will, in a moment." Bethell took out a handkerchief and mopped his forehead. "I say, don't you think it is warm in here ? Or is it only because I have been working hard? I'm going to let a little air in, before we start talking."

He walked to the window and threw it open. He leaned out for a moment, sniffing the cool breeze that blew from the river, then turned to the other two men.

"It was that time that I exclaimed 'Futhark', (which isn't a swear-word, by the way) that I got my idea," he said. "I'm pretty certain that the person to whom Raikes wrote that letter was . . ."

Crack!

A vivid spurt of flame flashed in the darkness beyond the open window. Bethell threw out his hands with an inarticulate cry, and collapsed to the floor.

MacNair and Lampson, carefully avoiding the window, sprang to the fallen man and knelt by him.

"It's only in the shoulder, but it may be serious," said the detective, after a hurried scrutiny. "You look after him, Lampers. I'm going to catch this humorist."

In a moment he was at the front door. Jevons, who had heard the shot, was already there.

"Shut the door," snapped MacNair. "Don't make a target of yourself against the light. Now then, where is he?"

The two men peered into the night. Against the background of the trees a distant figure could just be discerned, running across the grass. The detectives started in pursuit.

CHAPTER EIGHTEEN

The pursued man, keeping well in the shadow of the trees, was seen to alter his course slightly, and turn away from the river. A moment later he was out of sight behind some stables.

"He's making for the gate," said MacNair. "Come on!"

When they arrived, panting, at the wide entrance gates, they found only a gatekeeper in his shirt sleeves, enjoying the cool evening on the steps of his little lodge. The road beyond was empty, save for a taxi, that rounded the corner and disappeared as they looked.

"Anybody been through?" MacNair asked.

The gatekeeper removed his pipe from his lips slowly and thoughtfully. "There was one of the young gents," he replied. "Don't know his name. He come out 'arf an hour ago and talked for a bit to an old man with whiskers, what come in a cab. Then old whiskers drives off, and the young gent goes back to the 'ouse. Then he comes back again just now, starts off down the road, without no 'at or coat, picks up a cab, and off he goes."

MacNair was already half-way up the street. As he ran, he called over his shoulder: "Where did he say to go to—did you hear?"

"He shouted 'Liverpool Street!' fit to wake the 'ole road," called the man in reply.

A few hundred yards further on, they were lucky enough to find an empty taxi. The cab in front could again be seen, turning into the busy Ranelingham Road.

"Follow that taxi in front," gasped MacNair, as he and Jevons tumbled in and the vehicle set off at a good pace.

"What's up?" said Jevons, when he had regained his breath.

In a few words MacNair told him of the deciphered letter and the shot through the window. "I expect he arranged a rendezvous with his old scoundrel of an uncle. Liverpool Street was just a bit of eye-wash for our benefit. They will probably try to bolt to the Continent."

They had emerged from a tangle of minor streets into which they had plunged, and were now in King's Road. Progress was slow, owing to the buses which lumbered with maddening slowness in front of them, but the taxi which they were pursuing was in a like plight, only a hundred yards ahead.

"But who's the chap we are chasing?" Jevons asked.

"Bethell was just going to tell me. He paid for that, poor chap. I fancy it's Lloyd—nice lot of uncles he has—but you can't be sure."

They had now come into Sloane Square; the pursued taxi kept straight on, and from Cliveden Place gained the wide, ill-lit emptiness of Eaton Square.

"Not Victoria, as I thought," said MacNair. "Perhaps it's Liverpool Street after all."

The leading taxi rattled along Hobart Place, and swung into Buckingham Palace Road. There was a sudden jarring of brakes, and MacNair's cab jerked to a standstill. A small two-seater, charging unexpectedly out of Palace Street, had narrowly missed crashing into them. A lurid outburst of gore-bespangled profanity from the taxidriver was cut short by MacNair.

"Shut up and get on," he snapped. "They'll get away."

The taxi ahead was fast disappearing into a tangle of traffic in the distance. They got clear of the two-seater, in which MacNair saw a frightened young man in evening clothes, and once more sped in pursuit. They came in sight of the taxi once more as they slid round the Victoria Memorial in front of the dark palace, and swept up the Mall. The lights of Trafalgar Square glowed far ahead.

"Look!" said Jevons suddenly, pointing. Over the top of the Admiralty Arch they could see the transmutograph in the Square.

"BOAT RACE MYSTERY," spelt the racing letters of fire. "MR. LEWIS BETHELL, COACH OF CAMBRIDGE CREW, WAS SHOT THIS EVENING. . . ."

MacNair smiled grimly. The leading taxi was now only fifty yards ahead, and it would certainly be held up in the slow roundabout of the gyratory traffic in Trafalgar Square, which at this hour was dense, as the theatres were about to raise their curtains.

The arch shot overhead. The taxi ahead turned left, but instead of following the tide of vehicles round the Square, it halted abruptly at the corner of Cockspur Street. A young man, hat-less, sprang out; MacNair could see the flash of the silver coins that he tossed to the driver before turning and plunging recklessly across the thronged roadway in the direction of the Strand. The two detectives quickly followed suit.

"I say," said Jevons, "there's a subway. Why not take that?"

"No good. We'd lose him," MacNair answered. Avoiding the onrushing taxis and buses, they dodged swiftly across to the central pavement, and jostled their way through the slow-footed crowds of pedestrians. The young man ahead cast a glance over his shoulder, and hurried on, across the roadway again.

Jevons gave an exclamation. "Good Lord! So that's who it is!"

"Yes, but don't stop to chat about it now," said MacNair roughly. "He's making for Charing Cross."

The young man now broke into a run, and pushed his way past startled porters into the station. MacNair was now close behind him; Jevons, an older man, was puffing in the rear. They were now in the central portion of the station. There were not many travellers at this hour; MacNair saw the young man glance rapidly to left and right, and then run towards a tall, elderly man, who apparently found a dark corner by the cloakroom the most suitable place in which to read his evening paper.

The man dropped his paper, and looked up. It was Raikes. At a word from the young man, he picked up the suit-case that stood beside him and trotted after him in the direction of the platforms.

Things now began to move swiftly. As the two emerged into the light, a burly man in a blue suit, an obvious plain-clothes policeman, glanced keenly at Raikes, then stepped forward. "William Raikes—" he began.

The hatless young man sprang in front of Raikes, and dealt the detective a vicious kick that sent him to the ground. With a cry of "This way!" he seized the old man's arm. Raikes dropped his suit-case, and the two clattered down the stairs that led to the Underground.

"Watch the other exit on the Strand, Jevons," cried MacNair. He dashed after the two men, but in a moment was engulfed in a crowd that eddied through the narrow passages and stairways of the tube. Dropping some coppers into an automatic machine selected at random, he secured a ticket, and crushed his way into a lift. His quarry was now lost to sight, and he had the choice of two platforms. Instinctively he chose the southbound; and, as he hurried to the platform, he was rewarded by the sight of Raikes stepping into the Kennington train that stood waiting. He had just time to leap into the nearest carriage before the train moved off.

At the first stop, which was Charing Cross—for the station he had left was, on the Underground system, called "Strand"—he alighted and looked along the line of opening doors. Raikes and the young man, whose carriage had halted opposite the exit, scuttled through the archway and up the steps, with MacNair close behind. He was forestalled at the escalator by a red-faced woman, who, puffing and panting, settled herself and a large brown-paper parcel on the step immediately in front of him, and resisted all his efforts to pass. He saw the hatless young man look cautiously round, then whisper something to his companion. They clambered up the moving stairs, and were again out of sight by the time the detective reached the top.

He found himself at a bewildering subterranean cross-roads, with travellers scurrying rabbit-like in every direction. Red lights, green lights, arrows and notice-boards summoned to every part of London: the Bakerloo to Piccadilly and Oxford Circus, the District Railway to Victoria and Earl's Court, the City and South London to Leicester Square and Tottenham Court Road, or to Waterloo and Morden. Which way had they gone?

"Seen a fat old man, white whiskers, and a young man with no hat?" he asked breathlessly of an official.

"No," snapped the man. "Yes—District westbound."

MacNair darted up the stairs to the left. There was no sign of his quarry on the platform, but an Inner Circle train was on the point of starting. He jumped in.

At Westminster he looked out. From a First Class carriage a little further ahead, the florid countenance of Raikes was cautiously protruded. MacNair felt like cheering; but he at once turned his head away. When he looked again, the old man and his companion were making for the exit.

"Now I've got you," he murmured.

The two pursued men, however, melted into the crowd ahead. MacNair looked about him. There were two exits: one straight ahead into Bridge Street, one along a passage leading to the Embankment. Which would they take? The first, probably. Stay—there was a third—the very thing, if there were no policeman on duty at this end, as he knew there probably would not be just then. He turned to the left, ignoring the swing-doors of the St. Stephens Club as out of the question,, and found himself at the entrance of the gloomy passage which led under Bridge Street to the Houses of Parliament. For the fugitives it would be easy enough to cut across Palace Yard, and lose themselves in the whirligig of Parliament Square. Sure enough, there in the distance were the two figures, one tall and bulky, the other shorter and slighter. He sprinted down the corridor after them.

The young man looked back and the two began to run. But, just as they reached the four steps and the iron gate which lead to the cloisters, a figure appeared coming towards them; that of a pompous-looking man, dressed in a top hat and spotless morning dress. As the two attempted to push past him, he halted squarely in the way at the top of the steps and extended his umbrella in a preposterous gesture of defiance.

"Are you aware," he began, "that this subway is reserved for Mem——"

He got no further. The young man swung his arm and dealt him a savage upper-cut that sent him reeling. But the delay was fatal. MacNair was upon them.

The young man turned with a snarl, and a wicked little automatic gleamed in his hand. Raikes, his great face white with terror, grasped his arm. "Not another!" he cried. "Two deaths is——"

A loud report reverberated through the tunnel, and the old man slumped to the floor with a groan. Before the youth could free his right hand from the dying man's clutch MacNair had sprung upon him and forced him against the wall. He wrenched the smoking pistol from his hand, and, panting, stood staring at his stocky, square-headed prisoner. A policeman from Palace Yard, alarmed by the shooting, came running to his assistance.

"Well," gasped MacNair with a grin, "it will seem quite like old times to have you back. We have a nice little cell in Cannon Row quite handy for you, Mr. Robert Tatersale."

CHAPTER NINETEEN

A month later, four men sat at dinner in a London club. Lewis Bethell and Hugh Gawsell, who had now recovered from their injuries, were two of them. Major Lampson and Inspector MacNair made up the party.

"What I want to know," said the detective, "is how you deciphered that letter. Our experts said that it was a simple cipher, but very cumbrous, and almost impossible to read without the key. How did you read it, Bethell, and how did you know that Tatersale had anything to do with it?"

Bethell smiled. "It's awfully simple, really," he said. "The letter was written in a sort of Runic. When I saw those Tripos books in the reading-room, and remembered that Tatersale's studies included Anglo-Saxon and Norse antiquities, that put me on to him at once."

"But I thought Runic was written with queer angular characters?"

"So it is. Look here." Bethell took up the menu card, and began to write on the back.

"Here is the ordinary Runic alphabet," he said, pushing the card to MacNair. This is what he had written:

F U TH A R K G W

H N I J ? P Z S

T B E M L NG D O

"I have written the equivalent English letters at the side," he explained. "I don't think anybody is certain what the letter after J is. Now, you will see that this alphabet, which is called Futhark, from the first six letters——"

"That's the word you shouted that night," interrupted Lampson.

"Yes. If you had been clever, you would have seen the point at once. As I was saying, the alphabet is always arranged in three groups of eight letters. The first group is called Frey's Eight. I forget what the other two are.

"There was also a sort of hieratic Runic, which served as a code and was used by priests. This was sometimes written in the form of rows of little Christmas trees, or barbed arrows if you like. The number of barbs on the left side indicated the number of the group, the number of barbs on the right indicated the number of the letter in the group. For instance—" he took up his pencil again "—the symbol ᛘ would indicate A. One barb on the left for the first group, and four barbs on the right for the fourth letter. Thus, my own name, in ordinary Runic characters, would be written

ᛒᛘᚹᛘᚾᚾ

In the code-Runic, it would become ᚯ ᚯᚦᚯᚯᚯ

"Sometimes, instead of drawing Christmas trees they used dots, the top dots for the group, the lower dots for the letter. So my name would be written

```
 . .      . .     .       . .       . .      . . "
 . .    . .  . .      . .      . . . .     . . . .
```

"Yes, but what's this got to do with the code letter?" asked Lampson.

"Wait a bit. Suppose, instead of dots, you used Arabic figures, and wrote the name in the form of a series of fractions, thus:

$$\frac{3}{2} \quad \frac{3}{3} \quad \frac{1}{3} \quad \frac{3}{3} \quad \frac{3}{5} \quad \frac{3}{5}$$

But why even do that ? Why not write it all in a row:

323313333535?"

"I begin to see it," MacNair murmured.

"You remember that quick brown fox?" Bethell went on. "It was arranged in five groups of five letters, like this:

T I O J A
H C W M Z
E K N P Y
Q B F S D
U R X L G

I should have spotted its similarity to the Futhark alphabet at once, but I was too dense. But when I did see the idea, I said to myself, 'this arrangement of letters takes in every letter of the alphabet except V, and no doubt U is used for V. Therefore, the probability is that it's a sort of Futhark. 15 should equal A, and so on.' So I tried it. I started off with 'My de . . .' That looked all right. But then came a 6, and I simply didn't know what to do with it, because there are only five groups, and five letters in each group."

He turned to Lampson. "You remember, I said to you that the numbers from 6 upwards were much scarcer than the others, and we wondered why. Well, I puzzled at the thing, and at last I saw the ridiculous truth. *All the numbers above 5 are simply blinds.*"

"I don't understand," said Lampson.

"Don't you? The figures 1 to 5 are the only ones that matter. The others have absolutely nothing to do with the cipher at all. They are simply stuck in at random to puzzle people who don't know the secret. In deciphering the code, when you come to a 6, 7, 8, 9 or o you just ignore it. Raikes, of course, made a mistake in putting in too few of these blind numbers. They drew attention to themselves by their scarcity."

"I expect he found it too much of a sweat," observed Gawsell.

"I dare say he did. The code was undoubtedly Tatersale's invention. The beauty of it is that even a man who understood the system would be at sea without the key. You could vary the grouping of your key, or Futhark, almost indefinitely. You might, for instance, have three groups of eight letters, as in the original Runic, or four groups of six letters, with a couple extra in one group, or any way you like."

Lampson shook his head. "You may call it simple, old boy," he said, "but it strikes me as worse than the Income Tax. . . . But, tell me, Angus. Why exactly did he do it, and how? I've never been able to get the hang of that yet."

"I had better begin at the beginning," said MacNair. "Old Raikes was Tatersale's mother's brother. Those three are the only members of the family, as far as I know. Tatersale's father died ten years ago, and Raikes, who never married, was always very fond of his nephew. A few years ago, Raikes got acquainted with the Straylers, father and son. There was all this money, which couldn't be touched except through the boy. Their precious scheme to buy the father's life interest in the estate fell through. What does old Raikes do? He persuades the son to insure his life for a very big sum, and to make over the insurance money to him. I suppose he pitched him some yarn about repaying him, Raikes, for all he had done for the Straylers in case Alan should die before he came of age and could break the entail. Also, he somehow persuaded him not to tell his father of this.

"The idea of killing him was very likely Robert Tatersale's. He was hand in glove with his uncle, and they were both pretty thorough-paced scamps. I suppose they feared that when Alan came of age they might not get as much pickings from the estate as they hoped for. So they determined to kill him for the insurance—not knowing, apparently, that it was quite contrary to law for Alan to assign the money to Raikes. It reminds me very much of the Hamborough Case, in 1890, or thereabouts.

"Robert was to do the murder, since he would have ample opportunity. Raikes was to be kept out of it entirely. In fact, I don't think Alan Strayler ever knew that Tatersale and Raikes were any relation to each other, or even knew each other.

"Tatersale, I imagine, had devised some scheme for murdering Alan. What it was we shall never know. Then, one day down at the boat-house, a chance incident gave him a really brainy idea. It was when Owen Lloyd quite innocently asked him to throw him a tool. He was at once reminded of the theme of a detective story, *The Rasp,* which he knew had been lying about the house quite recently. Perhaps Lloyd had read it, perhaps he never did. I don't know. Anyway, what Tatersale did was this. He took the spanner up to the house, *and killed Strayler in exactly the way that I described to you,* a day or two after it happened."

Lampson sat open-mouthed. "But—but—" he mumbled.

"Wait a bit," said MacNair. "Robert Tatersale deliberately cast suspicion on himself. Why? Because the death had to be assumed to be murder or accident. If it were suicide, the insurance people wouldn't pay up. So he made the evidence point to *himself.* He wanted to be suspected, even arrested, because he knew that the case against him was impossibly weak. But he went a step further. He knew, or rather hoped, that some bright person would say: 'Aha! Somebody else killed Alan, and cast suspicion on poor old Tatersale, by monkeying with finger-prints on the handle of the spanner.' It was sheer luck for Tatersale that Dursfield saw the incident in the boat-house. But even if he hadn't, Robert was ready to insinuate the idea into my innocent ears. In fact, my artless questions simply presented him with what he wanted on a silver platter, so to speak. There I was, all eager to suspect Lloyd—and that was just what he wanted me to do."

"But really, this is too far-fetched," protested Bethell. " Suppose nobody had been brainy enough to think of this *Rasp* business. Where would Tatersale be then?"

"That would have been still all right for him. He would have stood his trial. The Raikes and insurance part of the story would never be connected with him. Nobody knew that Raikes was his uncle; they both kept that as dark as they could. So the case against Robert would have been very weak—and he would have been acquitted. Once acquitted, he would be safe; we might find out about his uncle, but he could snap his fingers at us. The law couldn't touch him."

"But why did he shoot Lewis ?" asked Lampson. "Of course, I can understand him hitting cox on the head. I only wonder I didn't do it myself."

"He made a statement after he was arrested," answered MacNair. "He was so broken up at having accidentally shot his uncle that he confessed the whole bag of tricks.

"When he heard that his uncle had come to Ranelingham, he was furious. He wanted the old man to keep right in the background, of course. So, when he got a chance, he telephoned to Raikes at the hotel he usually stayed at. He cursed him pretty freely, I expect. But Raikes said he must see him. So it was arranged that Raikes should come to the gates at eight o'clock that evening. Robert went down to meet him, and talked to him. He said that things were not going well. You, cox, he suspected of having guessed the truth."

"So I did," Gawsell interrupted. "I tried to tell Horace and Lewis, but they kicked me out of the room."

"So Robert, like gentle Alice Brown in the *Bab Ballads,* took a life preserver and hit you on the head. Anyway, he told his uncle that he was afraid things might go wrong, and that both of them might have to bolt. But he didn't want to bolt till he was sure the game was up. They had nowhere to bolt to, and no money to speak of. So he arranged to go back to the house. Raikes, meanwhile, was to be at Charing Cross Station between eight-thirty and nine, where they would meet in case of necessity. They had no definite plans. They couldn't bolt straight to the Continent, as they had no passports and had made no arrangements. I imagine they merely intended to slip off somewhere, lie low for a bit, and then leave the country when they could.

"Just before they parted, Raikes insisted on slipping a pistol into Tatersale's pocket, in case of emergency. So Robert came back to the house. He was alarmed to see us three nosing about and acting suspiciously, and he hung about in the grounds outside the reading-room. Then you, Bethell, most imprudently opened the window just before you began to blow the gaff. So he took a pot-shot at you, and bolted. And that's that."

"I still don't see," complained Lampson, "how he could have hoped to conceal his relationship to Raikes, and the connexion between Alan's murder and the life insurance, if he had stood his trial. Surely the mere fact that you did discover the whole plot knocks that theory on the head."

"We only got on to it by luck," MacNair protested. "Tatersale made two bad slips. In the first place, he failed to make sure that the incriminating letter from his uncle was properly burnt. In the second place, he left the key to the code where cox found it. What happened, I suppose, was this. He got a letter, one of many no doubt, from his uncle; perhaps he was writing a letter himself; I don't know which. As an aid to his coding or decoding, whichever it was, he scribbled the 'quick brown fox' key-pattern in the back of a novel he was reading. He erased it as soon as he had done with it, and of course assumed that the book would be taken back to the library in due course. He should have been more careful to destroy every scrap of paper that he used for this purpose. Then Raikes made a bad mistake in coming to Putney out of curiosity. He wanted to find out, I suppose, whether we had discovered the whole plot when we first arrested Tatersale. He should never have stirred from Whitby.

"Robert Tatersale's early life was spent in London, I have discovered. It was only at the death of his father that his mother took a small place in Dorset. They were strangers there, and none of the neighbours knew anything about the family, or about the uncle in Yorkshire. Mrs. Tatersale, by the way, knew absolutely nothing about this plot, poor woman. She only knew that Robert occasionally saw his uncle, when the latter came up to London on business or on holiday. Robert used to come to town and spend a day or two with him; and it is certain that Raikes never mentioned 'my nephew at Cambridge' to either of the Straylers. Robert said in his confession that he had not been to Whitby since he was a small schoolboy."

"There's one thing that puzzles me," said Gawsell suddenly. "How did Robert lock the bathroom door on the inside?"

"He didn't. He locked it on the outside. You remember that he was one of the first to enter the room when the door was broken down. The key was in his pocket; as soon as he got a chance, he slipped it on the floor under the wreckage of the door. As for the spanner, he simply threw it into the bushes, with his own finger-prints all over it. The handle you found that day—and which the excellent Jevons was looking everywhere for, by the way—he himself hid, expecting us to believe, as we did, that Lloyd had used it when he struck Alan with the spanner, and had then substituted the handle which bore Tatersale's finger-prints."

"Why did he pick Lloyd as scape-goat?" asked Lampson.

"Probably Lloyd, in an unguarded moment, told him about his uncle's ridiculous will, according to which he lost £1,000 if he did not row in the Boat Race. Robert knew that we should find out about the will sooner or later."

"But, look here." Bethell leaned forward earnestly. "It would have been to the advantage of Raikes and Tatersale to keep Alan alive until he was twenty-one, since they could have got all the money they wanted then. But, even assuming that they were fools enough to go for the insurance money, which they wouldn't have got anyhow, why on earth should Robert not wait until after the Boat Race ? After all, he was President of the C.U.B.C. He may be a scoundrel, but he was a keen enough rowing man, one would think, to avoid any scheme that would dish his own Boat Race."

MacNair sipped his port reflectively before replying: "I think you have answered your own question," he said. "This was no mere affair of hatred or revenge. It was a cold-blooded, calculated crime. At any sacrifice, everything must be, fool-proof. Naturally, people would say what you have just said: no President would deliberately muck up his Boat Race like that; however much he hated his stroke, he would wait for his revenge until the race was over. So, for security's sake, and for the sake of his share of the, £20,000, he sacrificed the Boat Race."

Hugh Gawsell leaned back in his chair and puffed at a cigarette. "Do you know," he began, "I think there's something deeper behind all this. I think Robert's confession is just spoof. He's shielding somebody. I have my suspicions of ——"

"SHUT UP, COX!"

Several elderly members of the Senior University Club were scandalised to see one of their most respected fellow-members, Major Horace Lampson, take up a hard roll and fling it with force and accuracy at the head of one of his guests.